D0337462

SALOME

by
OSCAR WILDE

UNDER THE HILL

by
AUBREY BEARDSLEY

SALOME
by
Oscar Wilde
First published 1894
UNDER THE HILL
by
Aubrey Beardsley
First published 1894
This compendium edition published 1996
by
Creation Books
83 Clerkenwell Road
London EC1, UK
Copyright © Creation Books 1996
A Creation Books Artefact
Creation Classics VI
ISBN 1 871592 12 7
Cover illustration:
"John And Salome"
by
Aubrey Beardsley
Design:
Bradley Davis

CONTENTS

FOREWORD

Censored, banned, and ridiculed upon publication, Oscar Wilde's *Salome*, written in 1892 in the French language, must now be viewed as one of the greatest of all Decadent texts; an Æsthetic masterwork which has seldom been accorded due respect.

The reasons for *Salome*'s prohibition are obvious: blasphemies abound; more than this, its atmosphere seethes with a dangerous erotic charge from the very outset. Relentless, hypnotic repetitions in the words, arranged in fugue cadences, lend the proceedings a masturbatory, oneiric quality; excepting a brief digression in which theological absurdities are dissected, the tale unfolds with the inexorable acceleration of an orgasmic nightmare. Forsaking his usual epigrammatic style, Wilde instead enriches his concentric vision with jewels piled upon jewels of quintessential exotica; weaving his tale on different levels, blurring reality through extended similes between the human and the elemental, as his exquisite damnation ritual is played out by deliberate archetypes. Salome herself, ostensibly the arch *femme fatale*, becomes interchangeable with the moon. The moon is loaded with deadly fate, and the Angel of Death presides over the entire assembly. Iokanaan rises, returns, and rises again, undead, from the Pit, as Nature runs amok; fabulous treasures are nulled, made worthless by the grey, bitter ashes of Love.

Here lies the fulcrum of Wilde's onslaught against Christianity, through which Salome is revealed not as sinner, but victim; not only lusted after by Herod but reviled as evil and repellent by Christ's harbinger, Iokanaan. As a spokesman for this duplicitous religion, Iokanaan personifies its hideous misogyny; his tirades against both Salome and her mother illustrating the Christian fear of Nature, its cycles, its chaos and its fertility, as embodied in womankind. Whereas the young Syrian sees only beauty and gentleness in Salome, the Prophet finds a deadly threat of emasculation.

The text itself is threaded with motifs of flesh, fresh blood, and the void itself. Even sounds, thoughts, are cast in silvers, reds and blacks. In the correlation between Salome, the moon, and the blood which seems to symbolise the breaking of hymens, menstruation, and male castration, there is a rampant suggestion of vampirism, even cannibalism. Oral gratification is sought above all. The protagonists are uniformly obsessive; oblivious to the constant strophe and antistrophe of incestuous desires, jealousies and entreaties, contradictions and maledictions. Almost total immorality pervades, and ironically it is only King Herod, the traditional tyrant, who finally rails for justice in the fallen order — having instigated its collapse through his own fear and lust. The drama spirals to its inevitable climax: sexual fury finds its catharsis in death upon violent death, and the audience, at first mesmerized, then dazzled, then horrified, are spent.

Aubrey Beardsley's *Under The Hill*, another work of pure decadence and sexual excess, includes such activities as shoe fetishism, bestiality, orgies, paedophilia, all manner of oral sex and homosexuality, sex with dwarfs and satyrs, onanism, sodomy, the eating of ear wax and the quaffing of saliva, menstrual blood and unicorn semen – yet all couched in such extravagant, perfumed language that far from being offensive, the text has more of the effect of an erotic dream from which the reader is loathe to awaken.

A short work left unfinished at the time of Beardsley's premature demise, *Under The Hill* nonetheless achieves the quintessence of Decadence, and in its evocation of a synaesthetic pleasure dome is surely the equal of Huysmans' *A Rebours*. This, allied to the extraordinary catalogue of sexual perversion detailed above, makes it a unique and indispensable text for any who seek the uttermost extremes of the manifest imagination.

This joint centennial edition of *Salome* and *Under The Hill*, united by seventeen of Beardsley's unsurpassable drawings, is an attempt to rehabilitate these two all-too-often ignored texts, and in so doing present a volume of unadulterated Decadent erotica which must surely stand as the apogee of its kind.

— **James Havoc**, Series Editor, 1994.

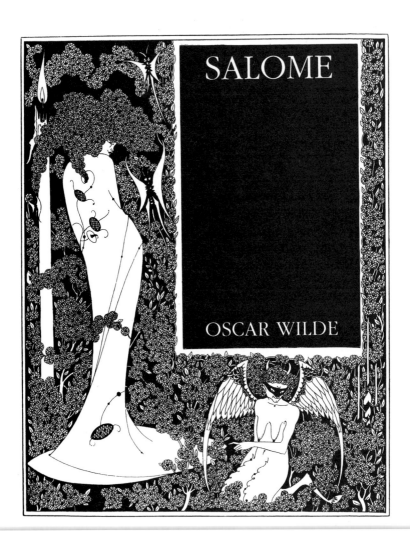

SALOME

A Tragedy In One Act
by
OSCAR WILDE

Translated
from the French
by
Lord Alfred Douglas

Pictured
by
AUBREY BEARDSLEY

THE PERSONS OF THE PLAY

HEROD ANTIPAS, TETRARCH OF JUDÆA
IOKANAAN, THE PROPHET
THE YOUNG SYRIAN, CAPTAIN OF THE GUARD
TIGELLINUS, A YOUNG ROMAN
A CAPPADOCIAN
A NUBIAN
FIRST SOLDIER
SECOND SOLDIER
THE PAGE OF HERODIAS
JEWS, NAZARENES, ETC.
A SLAVE
NAAMAN, THE EXECUTIONER
HERODIAS, WIFE OF THE TETRARCH
SALOME, DAUGHTER OF HERODIAS
THE SLAVES OF SALOME

SCENE — A great terrace in the Palace of Herod, set above the banqueting-hall. Some soldiers are leaning over the balcony. To the right there is a gigantic staircase, to the left, at the back, an old cistern surrounded by a wall of green bronze. The moon is shining very brightly.

THE YOUNG SYRIAN: How beautiful is the Princess Salome tonight!

THE PAGE OF HERODIAS: Look at the moon. How strange the moon seems! She is like a woman rising from a tomb. She is like a dead woman. One might fancy she was looking for dead things.

THE YOUNG SYRIAN: She has a strange look. She is like a little princess who wears a yellow veil, and whose feet are of silver. She is like a princess who has little white doves for feet. One might fancy she was dancing.

THE PAGE OF HERODIAS: She is like a woman who is dead. She moves very slowly. *[Noise in the banqueting-hall]*

FIRST SOLDIER: What an uproar! Who are those wild beasts howling?

SECOND SOLDIER: The Jews. They are always like that. They are disputing about their religion.

FIRST SOLDIER: Why do they dispute about their religion?

SECOND SOLDIER: I cannot tell. They are always doing it. The Pharisees, for instance, say that there are angels, and the Sadducees declare that angels do not exist.

FIRST SOLDIER: I think it is ridiculous to dispute about such things.

THE YOUNG SYRIAN: How beautiful is the Princess Salome tonight!

THE PAGE OF HERODIAS: You are always looking at her. You look at her too much. It is dangerous to look at people in such fashion. Something terrible may happen.

THE YOUNG SYRIAN: She is very beautiful tonight.

FIRST SOLDIER: The Tetrarch has a sombre aspect.

SECOND SOLDIER: Yes; he has a sombre aspect.

FIRST SOLDIER: He is looking at something.

SECOND SOLDIER: He is looking at some one.

FIRST SOLDIER: At whom is he looking?

SECOND SOLDIER: I cannot tell.

THE YOUNG SYRIAN: How pale the Princess is! Never have I seen her so pale. She is like the shadow of a white rose in a mirror of silver.

THE PAGE OF HERODIAS: You must not look at her. You look too much at her.

FIRST SOLDIER: Herodias has filled the cup of the Tetrarch.

THE CAPPADOCIAN: Is that the Queen Herodias, she who wears a black mitre sewed with pearls, and whose hair is powdered with blue dust?

FIRST SOLDIER: Yes; that is Herodias, the Tetrarch's wife.

SECOND SOLDIER: The Tetrarch is very fond of wine. He has wine of three sorts. One which is brought from the Island of Samothrace, and is purple like the cloak of Cæsar.

THE CAPPADOCIAN: I have never seen Cæsar.

SECOND SOLDIER: Another that comes from a town called Cyprus, and is as yellow as gold.

THE CAPPADOCIAN: I love gold.

SECOND SOLDIER: And the third is a wine of Sicily. That wine is red as blood.

THE NUBIAN: The gods of my country are very fond of blood. Twice in the year we sacrifice to them young men and maidens; fifty young men and a hundred maidens. But I am afraid that we never give them quite enough, for they are very harsh to us.

THE CAPPADOCIAN: In my country there are no gods left. The Romans have driven them out. There are some who say that they have hidden themselves in the mountains, but I do not believe it. Three nights I have been on the mountains seeking them everywhere. I did not find them, and at last I called them by their names, and they did not come. I think they are dead.

FIRST SOLDIER: The Jews worship a God that one cannot see.

THE CAPPADOCIAN: I cannot understand that.

FIRST SOLDIER: In fact, they only believe in things that one cannot see.

THE CAPPADOCIAN: That seems to me altogether ridiculous.

THE VOICE OF IOKANAAN: After me shall come another mightier than I. I am not worthy so much as to unloose the latchet of his shoes. When he cometh the solitary places shall be glad. They shall blossom like the rose. The eyes of the blind shall see the day, and the ears of the deaf shall be opened. The sucking child shall put his hand upon the dragon's lair, he shall lead the lions by their manes.

SECOND SOLDIER: Make him be silent. He is always saying ridiculous things.

FIRST SOLDIER: No, no. He is a holy man. He is very gentle, too. Every day when I give him to eat he thanks me.

THE CAPPADOCIAN: Who is he?

FIRST SOLDIER: A prophet.

THE CAPPADOCIAN: What is his name?

FIRST SOLDIER: Iokanaan.

THE CAPPADOCIAN: Whence comes he?

FIRST SOLDIER: From the desert, where he fed on locusts and wild honey. He was clothed in camel's hair, and round his loins he had a leathern belt. He was very terrible to look upon. A great multitude used to follow him. He even had disciples.

THE CAPPADOCIAN: What is he talking of?

FIRST SOLDIER: We can never tell. Sometimes he says things that affright one, but it is impossible to understand what he says.

THE CAPPADOCIAN: May one see him?

FIRST SOLDIER: No. The Tetrarch has forbidden it.

THE YOUNG SYRIAN: The Princess has hidden her face behind her fan! Her little white hands are fluttering like doves that fly to their dove-cots. They are like white butterflies. They are just like white butterflies.

THE PAGE OF HERODIAS: What is that to you? Why do you look at her? You must not look at her... Something terrible may happen.

THE CAPPADOCIAN: *[Pointing to the cistern]* What a strange prison!

SECOND SOLDIER: It is an old cistern.

THE CAPPADOCIAN: An old cistern! That must be a poisonous place in which to dwell!

SECOND SOLDIER: Oh no! For instance, the Tetrarch's brother, his elder brother, the first husband of Herodias the Queen, was imprisoned there for twelve years. It did not kill him. At the end of twelve years he had to be strangled.

THE CAPPADOCIAN: Strangled? Who dared to do that?

SECOND SOLDIER: *[Pointing to the Executioner, a huge negro]* That man yonder, Naaman.

THE CAPPADOCIAN: He was not afraid?

SECOND SOLDIER: Oh no! The Tetrarch sent him the ring.

THE CAPPADOCIAN: What ring?

SECOND SOLDIER: The death ring. So he was not afraid.

THE CAPPADOCIAN: Yet it is a terrible thing to strangle a king.

FIRST SOLDIER: Why? Kings have but one neck, like other men.

THE CAPPADOCIAN: I think it is terrible.

THE YOUNG SYRIAN: The Princess is getting up! She is leaving the table! She looks very troubled. Ah, she is coming this way. Yes, she is coming towards us. How pale she is! Never have I seen her so pale.

THE PAGE OF HERODIAS: Do not look at her. I pray you not to look at her.

THE YOUNG SYRIAN: She is like a dove that has strayed... She is like a narcissus trembling in the wind... She is like a silver flower. *[Enter Salome]*

SALOME: I will not stay. I cannot stay. Why does the Tetrarch look at me all the while with his mole's eyes under his shaking eyelids? It is strange that the husband of my mother looks at me like that. I know not what it means. Of a truth I know it too well.

THE YOUNG SYRIAN: You have left the feast, Princess?

SALOME: How sweet is the air here! I can breathe here! Within there are Jews from Jerusalem who are tearing each other in pieces over their foolish ceremonies, and barbarians who drink and drink and spill their wine on the pavement, and Greeks from Smyrna with painted eyes and painted cheeks, and frizzed hair curled in columns, and Egyptians silent and subtle, with long nails of jade and russet cloaks, and Romans brutal and coarse, with their uncouth jargon. Ah! How I hate the Romans! They are rough and common, and they give themselves the airs of noble lords.

THE YOUNG SYRIAN: Will you be seated, Princess?

THE PAGE OF HERODIAS: Why do you speak to her? Oh! Something terrible will happen. Why do you look at her?

SALOME: How good to see the moon! She is like a little piece of money, a little silver flower. She is cold and chaste. I am sure she is a virgin. She has the beauty of a virgin. Yes, she is a virgin. She has never defiled herself. She has never abandoned herself to men, like the other goddesses.

THE VOICE OF IOKANAAN: Behold! The Lord hath come. The Son of Man is at hand. The centaurs have hidden themselves in the rivers, and the nymphs have left the rivers, and are lying beneath the leaves in the forests.

SALOME: Who was that who cried out?

SECOND SOLDIER: The prophet, Princess.

SALOME: Ah, the prophet! He of whom the Tetrarch is afraid?

SECOND SOLDIER: We know nothing of that, Princess. It was the prophet Iokanaan who cried out.

THE YOUNG SYRIAN: Is it your pleasure that I bid them bring your litter, Princess? The night is fair in the garden.

SALOME: He says terrible things about my mother, does he not?

SECOND SOLDIER: We never understand what he says, Princess.

SALOME: Yes; he says terrible things about her. *[Enter a slave]*

THE SLAVE: Princess, the Tetrarch prays you to return to the feast.

SALOME: I will not return.

THE YOUNG SYRIAN: Pardon me, Princess, but if you return not some misfortune may happen.

SALOME: Is he an old man, this prophet?

THE YOUNG SYRIAN: Princess, it were better to return. Suffer me to lead you in.

SALOME: This prophet... is he an old man?

FIRST SOLDIER: No, he is quite young.

SECOND SOLDIER: One cannot be sure. There are those who say he is Elias.

SALOME: Who is Elias?

SECOND SOLDIER: A prophet of this country in bygone days, Princess.

THE SLAVE: What answer may I give the Tetrarch from the Princess?

THE VOICE OF IOKANAAN: Rejoice not, O land of Palestine, because the rod of him who smote thee is broken. For from the seed of the serpent shall come a basilisk, and that which is born of it shall devour the birds.

SALOME: What a strange voice! I would speak with him.

FIRST SOLDIER: I fear it may not be, Princess. The Tetrarch does not suffer any one to speak with him. He has even forbidden the high priest to speak with him.

SALOME: I desire to speak with him.

FIRST SOLDIER: It is impossible, Princess.

SALOME: I will speak with him.

THE YOUNG SYRIAN: Would it not be better to return to the banquet?

SALOME: Bring forth this prophet. *[Exit the Slave]*

FIRST SOLDIER: We dare not, Princess.

SALOME: *[Approaching the cistern and looking down into it]* How black it is, down there! It must be terrible to be in so black a hole! It is like a tomb... *[To the soldiers]* Did you not hear me? Bring out the prophet. I would look on him.

SECOND SOLDIER: Princess, I beg you, do not require this of us.

SALOME: You are making me wait upon your pleasure.

FIRST SOLDIER: Princess, our lives belong to you, but we cannot do what you have asked of us. And indeed, it is not of us that you should ask this thing.

SALOME: *[Looking at the young Syrian]* Ah!

THE PAGE OF HERODIAS: Oh! what is going to happen? I am sure that something terrible will happen.

SALOME: *[Going up to the young Syrian]* Thou wilt do this thing for me, wilt thou not, Narraboth? Thou wilt do this thing for me. I have ever been kind towards thee. Thou wilt do it for me. I would but look at him, this strange prophet. Men have talked so much of him. Often I have heard the Tetrarch talk of him. I think he is afraid of him, the Tetrarch. Art thou, even thou, also afraid of him, Narraboth?

THE YOUNG SYRIAN: I fear him not, princess; there is no man I fear. But the Tetrarch has formally forbidden that any man should raise the cover of this well.

SALOME: Thou wilt do this thing for me, Narraboth, and tomorrow when I pass in my litter beneath the gateway of the idol-sellers I will let fall for thee a little flower, a little green flower.

THE YOUNG SYRIAN: Princess, I cannot, I cannot.

SALOME: *[Smiling]* Thou wilt do this thing for me, Narraboth. Thou knowest that thou wilt do this thing for me. And on the morrow when I shall pass in my litter by the bridge of the idol-buyers, I will look at thee through the muslin veils, I will look at thee, Narraboth, it may be I will smile at thee. Look at me, Narraboth, look at me. Ah! thou knowest that thou wilt do what I ask of thee. Thou knowest it... I know that thou wilt do this thing.

THE YOUNG SYRIAN: *[Signing to the third Soldier]* Let the prophet come forth... The Princess Salome desires to see him.

SALOME: Ah!

THE PAGE OF HERODIAS: Oh! How strange the moon looks! Like the hand of a dead woman who is seeking to cover herself with a shroud.

THE YOUNG SYRIAN: She has a strange aspect! She is like a

little princess, whose eyes are eyes of amber. Through the clouds of muslin she is smiling like a little princess *[The prophet comes out of the cistern. Salome looks at him and steps slowly back]*

IOKANAAN: Where is he whose cup of abominations is now full? Where is he, who in a robe of silver shall one day die in the face of all the people? Bid him come forth, that he may hear the voice of him who hath cried in the waste places and in the houses of kings.

SALOME: Of whom is he speaking?

THE YOUNG SYRIAN: No one can tell, Princess.

IOKANAAN: Where is she who saw the images of men painted on the walls, even the images of the Chaldæans painted with colours, and gave herself up unto the lust of her eyes, and sent ambassadors into the land of Chaldæa?

SALOME: It is of my mother that he is speaking.

THE YOUNG SYRIAN: Oh no, Princess?

SALOME: Yes: it is of my mother that he is speaking.

IOKANAAN: Where is she who gave herself unto the Captains of Assyria, who have many baldricks on their loins, and crowns of many colours on their heads? Where is she who hath given herself to the young men of the Egyptians, who are clothed in fine linen and hyacinth, whose shields are of gold, whose helmets are of silver, whose bodies are mighty? Go, bid her rise up from the bed of her abominations, from the bed of her incestuousness, that she may hear the words of him who prepareth the way of the Lord, that she may repent of her iniquities. Though she will not repent, but will stick fast in her abominations, go bid her come, for the fan of the Lord is in His hand.

SALOME: Ah, but he is terrible, he is terrible!

THE YOUNG SYRIAN: Do not stay here, Princess, I beseech you.

SALOME: It is his eyes above all that are terrible. They are like black holes burnt by torches in a tapestry of Tyre. They are like the black caverns where the dragons live, the black caverns of Egypt in which the dragons make their lairs. They are like black lakes troubled by fantastic moons... Do you think he will speak again?

THE YOUNG SYRIAN: Do not stay here, Princess. I pray you do not stay here.

SALOME: How wasted he is! He is like a thin ivory statue. He is like an image of silver. I am sure he is chaste, as the moon is. He is like a moonbeam, like a shaft of silver. His flesh must be very cold, cold as ivory... I would look closer at him.

THE YOUNG SYRIAN: No, no, Princess!

SALOME: I must look at him closer.

THE YOUNG SYRIAN: Princess! Princess!

IOKANAAN: Who is this woman who is looking at me? I will not have her look at me. Wherefore doth she look at me, with her golden eyes, under her gilded eyelids? I know not who she is. I do not desire to know who she is. Bid her begone. It is not to her that I would speak.

SALOME: I am Salome, daughter of Herodias, Princess of Judæa.

IOKANAAN: Back! daughter of Babylon! Come not near the chosen of the Lord. Thy mother hath filled the earth with the wine of her iniquities, and the cry of her sinning hath come up even to the ears of God.

SALOME: Speak again, Iokanaan. Thy voice is as music to mine ear.

THE YOUNG SYRIAN: Princess! Princess! Princess!

SALOME: Speak again! Speak again, Iokanaan, and tell me what I must do.

IOKANAAN: Daughter of Sodom, come not near me! But cover thy head with a veil, and scatter ashes upon thine head, and get thee to the desert, and seek out the Son of Man.

SALOME: Who is he, the Son of Man? Is he as beautiful as thou art, Iokanaan?

IOKANAAN: Get thee behind me! I hear in the palace the beating of the wings of the angel of death.

THE YOUNG SYRIAN: Princess, I beseech thee to go within.

IOKANAAN: Angel of the Lord God, what dost thou here with thy sword? Whom seekest thou in this palace? The day of him who shall die in a robe of silver has not yet come.

SALOME: Iokanaan!

IOKANAAN: Who speaketh?

SALOME: I am amorous of thy body, Iokanaan! Thy body is white, like the lilies of the field that the mower hath never mowed. Thy body is white like the snows that lie on the mountains of Judæa, and come down into the valleys. The roses in the garden of the Queen of Arabia are not so white as thy body. Neither the roses of the garden of the Queen of Arabia, the garden of spices of the Queen of Arabia, nor the feet of the dawn when they light on the leaves, nor the breast of the moon when she lies on the breast of the sea... There is nothing in the world so white as thy body. Suffer me to touch thy body.

IOKANAAN: Back! daughter of Babylon! By woman came evil into the world. Speak not to me. I will not listen to thee. I listen but to the voice of the Lord God.

SALOME: Thy body is hideous. It is like the body of a leper. It is like a plastered wall, where vipers have crawled; like a plastered wall where the scorpions have made their nest. It is like a whited sepulchre, full of loathsome things. It is horrible, thy body is horrible. It is of thy hair that I am enamoured, Iokanaan. Thy hair is like clusters of grapes, like the clusters of black grapes that hang from the vine-trees of Edom in the land of the Edomites. Thy hair is like the cedars of Lebanon, like the great cedars of Lebanon that give their shade to the lions and to the robbers who would hide in them by day. The long black nights, when the moon hides her face, when the stars are afraid, are not so black as thy hair. The silence that dwells in the forest is not so black. There is nothing in the world that is so black as thy hair... Suffer me to touch thy hair.

IOKANAAN: Back, daughter of Sodom! Touch me not. Profane not the temple of the Lord God.

SALOME: Thy hair is horrible. It is covered with mire and dust. It is like a crown of thorns placed on thy head. It is like a knot of serpents coiled round thy neck. I love not thy hair... It is thy mouth that I desire, Iokanaan. Thy mouth is like a band of scarlet on a tower of ivory. It is like a pomegranate cut in twain with a knife of ivory. The pomegranate flowers that blossom in the gardens of Tyre, and are redder than roses, are not so red. The red blasts of trumpets that herald the approach of kings, and make afraid the enemy, are not so red. Thy mouth is redder than the feet of those who tread the wine in the wine-press. It is redder than the feet of the doves who inhabit the temples and are fed by the priests. It is redder than the feet of him who cometh from a forest where he hath slain a lion, and seen gilded tigers. Thy mouth is like a branch of coral that fishers have found in the twilight of the sea, the coral that they keep for the kings!... It is like the vermilion that the Moabites find in the mines of Moab, the vermilion that the kings take from them. It is like the bow of the King of the Persians, that is painted with vermilion, and is tipped with coral. There is nothing in the world so red as thy mouth... Suffer me to kiss thy mouth.

IOKANAAN: Never! daughter of Babylon! daughter of Sodom! Never!

SALOME: I will kiss thy mouth, Iokanaan. I will kiss thy mouth.

THE YOUNG SYRIAN: Princess, Princess, thou who art like a garden of myrrh, thou who art the dove of all doves, look not at this man, look not at him! Do not speak such words to him. I cannot endure it... Princess, do not speak these things.

SALOME: I will kiss thy mouth, Iokanaan.

THE YOUNG SYRIAN: Ah! *[He kills himself, and falls between Salome and Iokanaan]*

THE PAGE OF HERODIAS: The young Syrian has slain himself! The young captain has slain himself! He has slain himself who was my friend! I gave him a little box of perfumes and ear-rings wrought in silver, and now he has killed himself! Ah, did he not say that some misfortune would happen? I, too, said it, and it has come to pass. Well I knew that the moon was seeking a dead thing, but I knew not that it was he whom she sought. Ah! why did I not hide him from the moon? If I had hidden him in a cavern she would not have seen him.

FIRST SOLDIER: Princess, the young captain has just slain himself.

SALOME: Suffer me to kiss thy mouth, Iokanaan.

IOKANAAN: Art thou not afraid, daughter of Herodias? Did I not tell thee that I heard in the palace the beating of the wings of the angel of death, and hath he not come, the angel of death?

SALOME: Suffer me to kiss thy mouth.

IOKANAAN: Daughter of adultery, there is but one who can save thee. It is He of whom I spake. Go seek Him. He is in a boat on the sea of Galilee, and He talketh with His disciples. Kneel down on the shore of the sea, and call unto Him by His name. When He cometh to thee, and to all who call on Him He cometh, bow thyself at His feet and ask of Him the remission of thy sins.

SALOME: Suffer me to kiss thy mouth.

IOKANAAN: Cursed be thou! daughter of an incestuous mother, be thou accursed!

SALOME: I will kiss thy mouth, Iokanaan.

IOKANAAN: I will not look at thee. Thou art accursed, Salome, thou art accursed. *[He goes down into the cistern]*

SALOME: I will kiss thy mouth, Iokanaan; I will kiss thy mouth.

FIRST SOLDIER: We must bear away the body to another place. The Tetrarch does not care to see dead bodies, save the bodies of those who he himself has slain.

THE PAGE OF HERODIAS: He was my brother, and nearer to me than a brother. I gave him a little box full of perfumes, and a ring of agate that he wore always on his hand. In the evening we were wont to walk by the river, and among the almond-trees, and he used to tell me of the things of his country. He spake ever very low. The sound of his voice was like the sound of a flute, of one who playeth upon the flute.

Also he had much joy to gaze at himself in the river. I used to reproach him for that.

SECOND SOLDIER: You are right; we must hide the body. The Tetrarch must not see it.

FIRST SOLDIER: The Tetrarch will not come to this place. He never comes on the terrace. He is too much afraid of the prophet. *[Enter Herod, Herodias, and all the court]*

HEROD: Where is Salome? Where is the Princess? Why did she not return to the banquet as I commanded her? Ah! there she is!

HERODIAS: You must not look at her! You are always looking at her!

HEROD: The moon has a strange look tonight. Has she not a strange look? She is like a mad woman, a mad woman who is seeking everywhere for lovers. She is naked too. She is quite naked. The clouds are seeking to clothe her nakedness, but she will not let them. She shows herself naked in the sky. She reels through the clouds like a drunken woman... I am sure she is looking for lovers. Does she not reel like a drunken woman? She is a mad woman, is she not?

HERODIAS: No; the moon is like the moon, that is all. Let us go within... We have nothing to do here.

HEROD: I will stay here! Manasseh, lay carpets there. Light torches. Bring forth the ivory tables, and the tables of jasper. The air here is sweet. I will drink more wine with my guests. We must show all honours to the ambassadors of Cæsar.

HERODIAS: It is not because of them that you remain.

HEROD: Yes; the air is very sweet. Come, Herodias, our guests await us. Ah! I have slipped! I have slipped in blood! It is an ill omen. It is a very ill omen. Wherefore is there blood here?... and this body, what does this body here? Think you I am like the King of Egypt, who gives no feast to his guests but that he shows them a corpse? Whose is it? I will not look on it.

FIRST SOLDIER: It is our captain, sire. It is the young Syrian whom you made captain of the guard but three days gone.

HEROD: I issued no order that he should be slain.

SECOND SOLDIER: He slew himself, sire.

HEROD: For what reason? I had made him captain of my guard!

SECOND SOLDIER: We do not know, sire. But with his own hand he slew himself.

HEROD: That seems strange to me. I had thought it was but the Roman philosophers who slew themselves. Is it not true, Tigellinus, that the philosophers at Rome slay themselves?

TIGELLINUS: There be some who slay themselves, sire. They are the Stoics. The Stoics are people of no cultivation. They are ridiculous people. I myself regard them as being perfectly ridiculous.

HEROD: I also. It is ridiculous to kill one's self.

TIGELLINUS: Everybody at Rome laughs at them. The Emperor has written a satire against them. It is recited everywhere.

HEROD: Ah! he has written a satire against them? Cæsar is wonderful. He can do everything... It is strange that the young Syrian has slain himself. I am sorry he has slain himself. I am very sorry. For he was fair to look upon. He was even very fair. He had languorous eyes. I remember that I saw that he looked languorously at Salome. Truly, I thought he looked too much at her.

HERODIAS: There are others who look too much at her.

HEROD: His father was a king. I drove him from his kingdom. And of his mother, who was a queen, you made a slave, Herodias. So he was here as my guest, as it were, and for that reason I made him my captain. I am sorry he is dead. Ho! why have you left the body here? It must be taken to some other place. I will not look at it — away with it! *[They take away the body]* It is cold here. There is a wind blowing. Is there not a wind blowing?

HERODIAS: No; there is no wind.

HEROD: I tell you there is a wind that blows... And I hear in the air something that is like the beating of wings, like the beating of vast wings. Do you not hear it?

HERODIAS: I hear nothing.

HEROD: I hear it no longer. But I heard it. It was the blowing of the wind. It has passed away. But no, I hear it again. Do you not hear it? It is just like a beating of wings.

HERODIAS: I tell you there is nothing. You are ill. Let us go within.

HEROD: I am not ill. It is your daughter who is sick to death. Never have I seen her so pale.

HERODIAS: I told you not to look at her.

HEROD: Pour me forth wine. *[Wine is brought]* Salome, come drink a little wine with me. I have here a wine that is exquisite. Cæsar himself sent it me. Dip into it thy little red lips, that I may drain the cup.

SALOME: I am not thirsty, Tetrarch.

HEROD: You hear how she answers me, this daughter of yours?

HERODIAS: She does right. Why are you always gazing at her?

HEROD: Bring me ripe fruits. *[Fruits are brought]* Salome, come and eat fruits with me. I love to see in a fruit the mark of thy little teeth. Bite but a little of this fruit, that I may eat what is left.

SALOME: I am not hungry, Tetrarch.

HEROD: *[To Herodias]* You see how you have brought up this daughter of yours.

HERODIAS: My daughter and I come of a royal race. As for thee, thy father was a camel driver! He was a thief and a robber to boot!

HEROD: Thou liest!

HERODIAS: Thou knowest well that it is true.

HEROD: Salome, come and sit next to me. I will give thee the throne of thy mother.

SALOME: I am not tired, Tetrarch.

HERODIAS: You see in what regard she holds you.

HEROD: Bring me — What is it that I desire? I forget. Ah! ah! I remember.

THE VOICE OF IOKANAAN: Behold the time is come! That which I foretold has come to pass. The day I spake of is at hand.

HERODIAS: Bid him be silent. I will not listen to his voice. This man is for ever hurling insults against me.

HEROD: He has said nothing against you. Besides, he is a very great prophet.

HERODIAS: I do not believe in prophets. Can a man tell what will come to pass? No man knows it. Also he is forever insulting me. But I think you are afraid of him... I know well that you are afraid of him.

HEROD: I am not afraid of him. I am afraid of no man.

HERODIAS: I tell you you are afraid of him. If you are not afraid of him why do you not deliver him to the Jews who for these six months past have been clamouring for him?

A JEW: Truly, my lord, it were better to deliver him into our hands.

HEROD: Enough on this subject. I have already given you my answer. I will not deliver him into your hands. He is a holy man. He is a man who has seen God.

A JEW: That cannot be. There is no man who hath seen God since the prophet Elias. He is the last man who saw God face to face. In these days God doth not show Himself. God hideth Himself. Therefore great evils have come upon the land.

ANOTHER JEW: Verily, no man knoweth if Elias the prophet did indeed see God. Peradventure it was but the shadow of God that he saw.

A THIRD JEW: God is at no times hidden. He showeth Himself at all times and in all places. God is in what is evil even as He is in what is good.

A FOURTH JEW: Thou shouldst not say that. It is a very dangerous doctrine. It is a doctrine that cometh from Alexandria, where men teach the philosophy of the Greeks. And the Greeks are Gentiles. They are not even circumcised.

A FIFTH JEW: No man can tell how God worketh. His ways are very dark. It may be that the things which we call evil are good, and the things which we call good are evil. There is no knowledge of anything. We can but bow our heads to His will, for God is very strong. He breaketh in pieces the strong together with the weak, for He regardeth not any man.

FIRST JEW: Thou speakest truly. Verily, God is terrible. He breaketh in pieces the strong and the weak as men break corn in a mortar. But as for this man, he hath never seen God. No man hath seen God since the prophet Elias.

HERODIAS: Make them be silent. They weary me.

HEROD: But I have heard it said that Iokanaan is in very truth your prophet Elias.

THE JEW: That cannot be. It is more than three hundred years since the days of the prophet Elias.

HEROD: There be some who say that man is Elias the prophet.

A NAZARENE: I am sure that he is Elias the prophet.

THE JEW: Nay, but he is not Elias the prophet.

THE VOICE OF IOKANAAN: Behold the day is at hand, the day of the Lord, and I hear upon the mountains the feet of Him who shall be the Saviour of the world.

HEROD: What does that mean? The Saviour of the world?

TIGELLINUS: It is a title that Cæsar adopts.

HEROD: But Cæsar is not coming into Judæa. Only yesterday I received letters from Rome. They contained nothing concerning this matter. And you, Tigellinus, who were at Rome during the winter, you heard nothing concerning this matter, did you?

TIGELLINUS: Sire, I heard nothing concerning the matter. I was but explaining the title. It is one of Cæsar's titles.

HEROD: But Cæsar cannot come. He is too gouty. They say that his feet are like the feet of an elephant. Also there are reasons of state. He who leaves Rome loses Rome. He will not come. Howbeit, Cæsar is lord, he will come if such be his pleasure. Nevertheless, I think he will not come.

FIRST NAZARENE: It was not concerning Cæsar that the prophet spake these words, sire.

HEROD: How? — it was not concerning Cæsar?

FIRST NAZARENE: No, my lord.

HEROD: Concerning whom then did he speak?

FIRST NAZARENE: Concerning Messias, who hath come.

A JEW: Messias hath not come.

FIRST NAZARENE: He hath come, and everywhere He worketh miracles!

HERODIAS: Ho! ho! miracles! I do not believe in miracles. I have seen too many. *[To the page]* My fan.

FIRST NAZARENE: This Man worketh true miracles. Thus, at a marriage which took place in a little town of Galilee, a town of some importance, He changed water into wine. Certain persons who were present related it to me. Also He healed two lepers that were seated before the Gate of Capernaum simply by touching them

SECOND NAZARENE: Nay; it was two blind men that He healed at Capernaum.

FIRST NAZARENE: Nay; they were lepers. But He hath healed blind people also, and He was seen on a mountain talking with angels.

A SADDUCEE: Angels do not exist.

A PHARISEE: Angels exist, but I do not believe that this Man has talked with them.

FIRST NAZARENE: He was seen by a great multitude of people talking with angels.

HERODIAS: How these men weary me! They are ridiculous! They are altogether ridiculous! *[To the Page]* Well! my fan? *[The Page gives her the fan]* You have a dreamer's look. You must not dream. It is only sick people who dream. *[She strikes the Page with her fan]*

SECOND NAZARENE: There is also the miracle of the daughter of Jairus.

FIRST NAZARENE: Yea, that is true. No man can gainsay it.

HERODIAS: Those men are mad. They have looked too long on the moon. Command them to be silent.

HEROD: What is this miracle of the daughter of Jairus?

FIRST NAZARENE: The daughter of Jairus was dead. This Man raised her from the dead.

HEROD: How! He raises people from the dead?

FIRST NAZARENE: Yea, sire; He raiseth the dead.

HEROD: I do not wish Him to do that. I forbid Him to do that. I suffer no man to raise the dead. This Man must be found and told that I forbid him to raise the dead. Where is this Man at present?

SECOND NAZARENE: He is in every place, my lord, but it is hard to find Him.

FIRST NAZARENE: It is said that He is now in Samaria.

A JEW: It is easy to see that this is not Messias, if He is in Samaria. It is not to the Samaritans that Messias shall come. The Samaritans are accursed. They bring no offerings to the Temple.

SECOND NAZARENE: He left Samaria a few days since. I think that at the present moment He is in the neighbourhood of Jerusalem.

FIRST NAZARENE: No; He is not there. I have just come from Jerusalem. For two months they have had no tidings of Him.

HEROD: No matter! But let them find Him, and tell Him, thus saith Herod the King, "I will not suffer Thee to raise the dead." To change water into wine, to heal the lepers and the blind... He may do these things if He will. I say nothing against these things. In truth I hold it a kindly deed to heal a leper. But no man shall raise the dead... It would be terrible if the dead came back.

THE VOICE OF IOKANAAN: Ah! the wanton one! the harlot! ah! the daughter of Babylon with her golden eyes and her gilded eyelids! Thus saith the Lord God, Let there come up against her a multitude of men. Let the people take stones and stone her...

HERODIAS: Command him to be silent!

THE VOICE OF IOKANAAN: Let the captains of the hosts pierce her with their swords, let them crush her beneath their shields.

HERODIAS: Nay, but it is infamous.

THE VOICE OF IOKANAAN: It is thus that I will wipe out all the wickedness from the earth, and that all women shall learn not to imitate her abominations.

HERODIAS: You hear what he says against me? You suffer him to revile her who is your wife!

HEROD: He did not speak your name.

HERODIAS: What does that matter? You know well that it is I whom he seeks to revile. And I am your wife, am I not?

HEROD: Of a truth, dear and noble Herodias, you are my wife, and before that you were the wife of my brother.

HERODIAS: It was thou didst snatch me from his arms.

HEROD: Of a truth I was stronger than he was... But let us not talk of that matter. I do not desire to talk of it. It is the cause of the terrible words the prophet has spoken. Peradventure on account of it a misfortune will come. Let us not speak of this matter. Noble Herodias, we are not mindful of our guests. Fill thou my cup, my well-beloved. Ho! fill with wine the great goblets of silver, and the great goblets of glass. I will drink to Cæsar. There are Romans here, we must drink to Cæsar.

ALL: Cæsar! Cæsar!

HEROD: Do you not see your daughter, how pale she is?

HERODIAS: What is it to you if she be pale or not?

HEROD: I have never seen her so pale.

HERODIAS: You must not look at her.

THE VOICE OF IOKANAAN: In that day the sun shall become black like sackcloth of hair, and the moon shall become like blood, and the stars of the heaven shall fall upon the earth like unripe figs that fall from the fig-tree, and the kings of the earth shall be afraid.

HERODIAS: Ah! ah! I should like to see that day of which he speaks, when the moon shall become like blood, and when the stars shall fall upon the earth like unripe figs. This prophet talks like a drunken man... but I cannot suffer the sound of his voice. I hate his voice. Command him to be silent.

HEROD: I will not. I cannot understand what it is that he saith, but it may be an omen.

HERODIAS: I do not believe in omens. He speaks like a drunken man.

HEROD: It may be he is drunk with the wine of God.

HERODIAS: What wine is that, the wine of God? From what vineyards is it gathered? In what winepress may one find it?

HEROD: *[From this point he looks all the while at Salome]* Tigellinus, when you were at Rome of late, did the Emperor speak with you on the subject of... ?

TIGELLINUS: On what subject, my lord?

HEROD: On what subject? Ah! I asked you a question, did I not? I have forgotten what I would have asked you.

HERODIAS: You are looking again at my daughter. You must not look at her. I have already said so.

HEROD: You say nothing else.

HERODIAS: I say it again.

HEROD: And that restoration of the Temple about which they have talked so much, will anything be done? They say that the veil of the Sanctuary has disappeared, do they not?

HERODIAS: It was thyself didst steal it. Thou speakest at random and without wit. I will not stay here. Let us go within.

HEROD: Dance for me, Salome.

HERODIAS: I will not have her dance.

SALOME: I have no desire to dance, Tetrarch.

HEROD: Salome, daughter of Herodias, dance for me.

HERODIAS: Peace. Let her alone.

HEROD: I command thee to dance, Salome.

SALOME: I will not dance, Tetrarch.

HERODIAS: *[Laughing]* You see how she obeys you.

HEROD: What is it to me whether she dances or not? It is nought to me. Tonight I am happy. I am exceeding happy. Never have I been so happy.

FIRST SOLDIER: The Tetrarch has a sombre look. Has he not a sombre look?

SECOND SOLDIER: Yes, he has a sombre look.

HEROD: Wherefore should I not be happy? Cæsar, who is lord of the world, Cæsar, who is lord of all things, loves me well. He has just sent me most precious gifts. Also he has promised me to summon to Rome the King of Cappadocia, who is mine enemy. It may be that at Rome he will crucify him, for he is able to do all things that he has a mind to do. Verily, Cæsar is lord. Therefore I do well to be happy. I am very happy, never have I been so happy. There is nothing in the world that can mar my happiness.

THE VOICE OF IOKANAAN: He shall be seated on his throne. He shall be clothed in scarlet and purple. In his hand he shall bear a golden cup full of his blasphemies. And the angel of the Lord shall smite him. He shall be eaten of worms.

HERODIAS: You hear what he says about you. He says you shall be eaten of worms.

HEROD: It is not of me that he speaks. He speaks never against me. It is of the King of Cappadocia that he speaks; the King of Cappadocia who is mine enemy. It is he who shall be eaten of worms. It is not I. Never has he spoken word against me, this prophet, save that I sinned in taking to wife the wife of my brother. It may be he is right. For, of a truth, you are sterile.

HERODIAS: I am sterile, I? You say that, you that are ever looking at my daughter, you that would have her dance for your pleasure? You speak as a fool. I have borne a child. You have gotten no child, no, not on one of your slaves. It is you who are sterile, not I.

HEROD: Peace, woman! I say that you are sterile. You have borne me no child, and the prophet says that our marriage is not a true marriage. He says that it is a marriage of incest, a marriage that will bring evils... I fear he is right; I am sure that he is right. But it is not the hour to speak of these things. I would be happy at this moment. Of a truth, I am happy. There is nothing I lack.

HERODIAS: I am glad you are of so fair a humour tonight. It is not your custom. But it is late. Let us go within. Do not forget that we hunt at sunrise. All honours must be shown to Cæsar's ambassadors, must they not?

SECOND SOLDIER: The Tetrarch has a sombre look.

FIRST SOLDIER: Yes, he has a sombre look.

HEROD: Salome, Salome, dance for me. I pray thee dance for me. I am sad tonight. Yes, I am passing sad tonight. When I came hither I slipped in blood, which is an ill omen; also I heard in the air a beating of wings, a beating of giant wings. I cannot tell what that may mean... I am sad tonight. Therefore dance for me. Dance for me, Salome, I beseech thee. If thou dancest for me thou mayest ask of me what thou wilt, and I will give it thee. Yes, dance for me, Salome, and whatsoever thou shalt ask of me I will give it thee, even unto the half my kingdom.

SALOME: *[Rising]* Will you indeed give me whatsoever I shall ask of you, Tetrarch?

HERODIAS: Do not dance, my daughter.

HEROD: Whatsoever thou shalt ask of me, even unto the half of my kingdom.

SALOME: You swear it, Tetrarch?

HEROD: I swear it, Salome.

HERODIAS: Do not dance, my daughter.

SALOME: By what will you swear this thing, Tetrarch?

HEROD: By my life, by my crown, by my gods. Whatsoever thou shalt desire I will give it thee, even to the half of my kingdom, if thou wilt but dance for me. O Salome, Salome, dance for me!

SALOME: You have sworn an oath, Tetrarch.

HEROD: I have sworn an oath.

HERODIAS: My daughter, do not dance.

HEROD: Even to the half of my kingdom. Thou wilt be passing fair as a queen, Salome, if it please thee to ask for the half of my kingdom. Will she not be fair as a queen? Ah! it is cold here! There is an icy wind, and I hear... wherefore do I hear in the air this beating of wings? Ah! one might fancy a huge, black bird that hovers over the terrace. Why can I not see it, this bird? The beat of its wings is terrible. The breath of the wind of its wings is terrible. It is a chill wind. Nay, but it is not cold, it is hot. I am choking. Pour water on my hands. Give me snow to eat. Loosen my mantle. Quick! quick! loosen my mantle. Nay, but leave it. It is my garland that hurts me, my garland of roses. The flowers are like fire. They have burned my forehead. *[He tears the wreath from his head, and throws it on the table]* Ah! I can breathe now. How red those petals are! They are like stains of blood on the cloth. That does not matter. It is not wise to find symbols in everything that one sees. It makes life too full of terrors. It were better to say that stains of blood are as lovely as rose-petals. It were better far to say that... But we will not speak of this. Now I am happy. I am passing happy. Have I not the right to be happy? Your daughter is going to dance for me. Wilt thou not dance for me, Salome? Thou hast promised to dance for me.

HERODIAS: I will not have her dance.

SALOME: I will dance for you, Tetrarch.

HEROD: You hear what your daughter says. She is going to dance for me. Thou doest well to dance for me, Salome. And when thou hast danced for me, forget not to ask of me whatsoever thou hast a mind to ask. Whatsoever thou shalt desire I will give it thee, even to the half of my kingdom. I have sworn it, have I not?

SALOME: Thou hast sworn it, Tetrarch.

HEROD: And I have never failed of my word. I am not of those who break their oaths. I know not how to lie. I am the slave of my word, and my word is the word of a king. The King of Cappadocia ever had a lying tongue, but he is no true king. He is a coward. Also he owes me money that he will not repay. He has even insulted my ambassadors. He has spoken words that were wounding. But Cæsar will crucify him when he comes to Rome. I know that Cæsar will crucify him. And if he crucify him not, yet will he die, being eaten of worms. The prophet has prophesied it. Well! Wherefore dost thou tarry, Salome?

SALOME: I am waiting until my slaves bring perfumes to me and the seven veils, and take from off my feet my sandals. *[Slaves bring perfumes and the seven veils, and take the sandals of Salome]*

HEROD: Ah, thou art to dance with naked feet! 'Tis well! 'tis well! Thy little feet will be like white doves. They will be like little white flowers that dance upon the trees... No, no, she is going to dance on blood! There is blood spilt on the ground. She must not dance on blood. It were an evil omen.

HERODIAS: What is it to thee if she dance on blood? Thou hast waded deep enough in it...

HEROD: What is it to me? Ah! look at the moon! She has become red. She has become red as blood. Ah! the prophet prophesied truly. He prophesied that the moon would become as blood. Did he not prophesy it? All of ye heard him prophesying it. And now the moon has become as blood. Do ye not see it?

HERODIAS: Oh yes, I see it well, and the stars are falling like unripe figs, are they not? And the sun is becoming black like sackcloth of hair, and the kings of the earth are afraid. That at least one can see. The prophet is justified of his words in that at least, for truly the kings of the earth are afraid... Let us go within. You are sick. They will say at Rome that you are mad. Let us go within, I tell you.

THE VOICE OF IOKANAAN: Who is this who cometh from Edom, who is this who cometh from Bozra, whose raiment is dyed with purple, who shineth in the beauty of his garments, who walketh mighty in his greatness? Wherefore is thy raiment stained with scarlet?

HERODIAS: Let us go within. The voice of that man maddens me. I will not have my daughter dance while he is continually crying out. I will not have her dance while you look at her in this fashion. In a word, I will not have her dance.

HEROD: Do not rise, my wife, my queen, it will avail thee nothing. I will not go within until she hath danced. Dance, Salome, dance for me.

HERODIAS: Do not dance, my daughter.

SALOME: I am ready, Tetrarch. *[Salome dances the dance of the seven veils]*

HEROD: Ah! wonderful! wonderful! You see that she has danced for me, your daughter. Come near, Salome, come near, that I may give thee thy fee. Ah! I pay a royal price to those who dance for my pleasure. I will pay thee royally. I will give thee whatsoever thy soul desireth. What wouldst thou have? Speak.

SALOME: *[Kneeling]* I would that they presently bring me in a silver charger...

HEROD: *[Laughing]* In a silver charger? Surely yes, in a silver charger. She is charming, is she not? What is it that thou wouldst have in a silver charger, O sweet and fair Salome, thou that art fairer than all the daughters of Judæa? What wouldst thou have them bring thee in a silver charger? Tell me. Whatsoever it may be, thou shalt receive it. My treasures belong to thee. What is it that thou wouldst have, Salome?

SALOME: *[Rising]* The head of Iokanaan.

HERODIAS: Ah! that is well said, my daughter.

HEROD: No, no!

HERODIAS: That is well said, my daughter.

HEROD: No, no, Salome. It is not that thou desirest. Do not listen to thy mother's voice. She is ever giving thee evil counsel. Do not heed her.

SALOME: It is not my mother's voice that I heed. It is for mine own pleasure that I ask the head of Iokanaan in a silver charger. You have sworn an oath, Herod. Forget not that you have sworn an oath.

HEROD: I know it. I have sworn an oath by my gods. I know it well. But I pray thee, Salome, ask of me something else. Ask of me the half of my kingdom, and I will give it thee. But ask not of me what thy lips have asked.

SALOME: I ask of you the head of Iokanaan.

HEROD: No, no, I will not give it thee.

SALOME: You have sworn an oath, Herod.

HERODIAS: Yes, you have sworn an oath. Everybody heard you. You swore it before everybody.

HEROD: Peace, woman! It is not to you I speak.

HERODIAS: My daughter has done well to ask the head of Iokanaan. He has covered me with insults. He has said unspeakable things against me. One can see that she loves her mother well. Do not yield, my daughter. He has sworn an oath, he has sworn an oath.

HEROD: Peace! I speak not to thee!... Salome, I pray thee be not stubborn. I have ever been kind toward thee. I have ever loved thee... It may be that I have loved thee too much. Therefore ask not this thing of me. This is a terrible thing, an awful thing to ask of me. Surely, I think thou art jesting. The head of a man that is cut from his body is ill to look upon, is it not? It is not meet that the eyes of a virgin should look upon such a thing. What pleasure couldst thou have in it? There is no pleasure that thou couldst have in it. No, no, it is not that thou desirest. Harken to me. I have an emerald, a great emerald and round, that the minion of Cæsar has sent unto me. When thou lookest through this emerald thou canst see that which passeth afar off. Cæsar himself carries such an emerald when he goes to the circus. But my emerald is the larger. It is the largest emerald in the whole world. Thou wilt take that, wilt thou not? Ask it of me and I will give it to thee.

SALOME: I demand the head of Iokanaan.

HEROD: Thou art not listening. Thou art not listening. Suffer me to speak, Salome.

SALOME: The head of Iokanaan!

HEROD: No, no, thou wouldst not have that. Thou sayest that but to trouble me, because that I have looked at thee and ceased not this night. It is true, I have looked at thee and ceased not this night. Thy beauty has troubled me. Thy beauty has grievously troubled me, and I have looked at thee overmuch. Nay, but I will look at thee no more. One should not look at anything. Neither at things, nor at people should one look. Only in mirrors is it well to look, for mirrors do but show us masks. Oh! oh! bring wine! I thirst... Salome, Salome, let us be as friends. Bethink thee... Ah! what would I say? What was't? Ah! I remember it!... Salome — nay, but come nearer to me; I fear thou wilt not hear my words — Salome, thou knowest my white peacocks, my beautiful white peacocks, that walk in the garden between the myrtles and the tall cypress-trees? Their beaks are gilded with gold and the grains that they eat are smeared with gold, and their feet are stained with purple. When they cry out the rain comes, and the moon shows herself in the heavens when they spread their tails. Two by two they walk between the cypress-trees and the black myrtles, and each has a slave to tend it. Sometimes they fly across the trees, and anon they couch in the grass, and round the pools of the water. There are not in all the world birds so wonderful. I know that Cæsar himself has no birds so fair as my birds. I will give thee fifty of my peacocks. They will follow thee whithersoever thou goest, and in the midst of them thou wilt be like unto the moon in the midst of a great white cloud... I will give them to thee, all. I have but a hundred, and in the whole world there is no king who has peacocks like unto my peacocks. But I will give them all to thee. Only thou must loose me from my oath, and must not ask of me that which thy lips have asked of me. *[He empties the cup of wine]*

SALOME: Give me the head of Iokanaan!

HERODIAS: Well said, my daughter! As for you, you are ridiculous with your peacocks.

HEROD: Peace! you are always crying out. You cry out like a beast of prey. You must not cry in such fashion. Your voice wearies me. Peace, I tell you!... Salome, think on what thou art doing. It may be that this man comes from God. He is a holy man. The finger of God has touched him. God has put terrible words into his mouth. In the palace, as in the desert, God is ever with him... It may be that He is, at least. One cannot tell, but it is possible that God is with him and for him. If he die also, peradventure some evil may befall me. Verily, he has said that evil will befall some one on the day whereon he dies. On whom should it fall if it fall not on me? Remember, I slipped in blood when I came hither. Also did I not hear a beating of wings in the air, a beating of vast wings? These are ill omens. And there were other things. I am sure that there were other things, though I saw them not. Thou wouldst not that some evil should befall me, Salome? Listen to me again.

SALOME: Give me the head of Iokanaan!

HEROD: Ah! thou art not listening to me. Be calm. As for me, am I not calm? I am altogether calm. Listen. I have jewels hidden in this place — jewels that thy mother even has never seen; jewels that are marvellous to look at. I have a collar of pearls, set in four rows. They are like unto moons chained with rays of silver. They are even as half a hundred moons caught in a golden net. On the ivory breast of a queen they have rested. Thou shalt be as fair as a queen when thou wearest them. I have amethysts of two kinds; one that is black like wine, and one that is red like wine that one has coloured with water. I have topazes yellow as are the eyes of tigers, and topazes that are pink as the eyes of a wood-pigeon, and green topazes that are as the eyes of cats. I have opals that burn always, with a flame that is cold as ice, opals that make sad men's minds, and are afraid of the shadows. I have onyxes like the eyeballs of a dead woman. I have moonstones that change when the moon changes, and are wan when they see the sun. I have sapphires big like eggs, and as blue as blue flowers. The sea wanders within them, and the moon comes never to trouble the blue of their waves. I have chrysolites and beryls, and chrysoprases and rubies; I have sardonyx and hyacinth stones, and stones of chalcedony, and I will give them all unto thee, all, and other things will I add to them. The King of the Indies has but even now sent me four fans fashioned from the feathers of parrots, and the King of Numidia a garment of ostrich feathers. I have a crystal, into which it is not lawful for a woman to look, nor may young men behold it until they have been beaten with rods. In a coffer of nacre I have three wondrous turquoises. He who wears them on his forehead can imagine things which are not, and he who carries them in his hand can turn the fruitful woman into a woman that is barren. These are great treasures. They are treasures above all price. But this is not all. In an ebony coffer I have two cups of amber that are like apples of pure gold. If an enemy pour poison into these cups they become like apples of silver. In a coffer incrusted with amber I have sandals incrusted with glass. I have mantles that have been brought from the land of the Seres, and bracelets decked about with carbuncles and with jade that come from the city of Euphrates... What desirest thou more than this, Salome? Tell me the thing that thou desirest, and I will give it thee. All that thou askest I will give thee, save one thing only. I will give thee all that is mine, save only the life of one man. I will give thee the mantle of the high priest. I will give thee the veil of the sanctuary.

THE JEWS: Oh! oh!

SALOME: Give me the head of Iokanaan!

HEROD: *[Sinking back in his seat]* Let her be given what she asks! Of a truth she is her mother's child! *[The first Soldier approaches. Herodias draws from the hand of the Tetrarch the ring of death, and gives it to the Soldier, who straightway bears it to the Executioner. The Executioner looks scared]* Who has taken my ring? There was a ring on my right hand. Who has drunk my wine? There was wine in my cup. It was full of wine. Some one has drunk it! Oh! surely some evil will befall some one. *[The Executioner goes down into the cistern]* Ah! wherefore did I give my oath? Hereafter let no king swear an oath. If he keep it not, it is terrible, and if he keep it, it is terrible also.

HERODIAS: My daughter has done well.

HEROD: I am sure that some misfortune will happen.

SALOME: *[She leans over the cistern and listens]* There is no sound. I hear nothing. Why does he not cry out, this man? Ah! if any man sought to kill me, I would cry out, I would struggle, I would not suffer... Strike, strike, Naaman, strike, I tell you... No, I hear nothing. There is a silence, a terrible silence. Ah! something has fallen upon the ground. I heard something fall. It was the sword of the Executioner. He is afraid, this slave. He has dropped his sword. He dares not kill him. He is a coward, this slave! Let soldiers be sent. *[She sees the Page of Herodias and addresses him]* Come hither. Thou wert the friend of him who is dead, wert thou not? Well, I tell thee, there are not dead men enough. Go to the soldiers and bid them go down and bring me the thing I ask, the thing the Tetrarch has promised me, the thing that is mine. *[The Page recoils. She turns to the soldiers]* Hither, ye soldiers. Get ye down into this cistern and bring me the head of this man. Tetrarch, Tetrarch, command your soldiers that they bring me the head of Iokanaan. *[A huge black arm, the arm of the Executioner, comes forth from the cistern, bearing on a silver shield the head of Iokanaan. Salome seizes it. Herod hides his face with his cloak. Herodias smiles and fans herself. The Nazarenes fall on their knees and begin to pray]* Ah! thou wouldst not suffer me to kiss thy mouth, Iokanaan. Well! I will kiss it now. I will bite it with my teeth as one bites a ripe fruit. Yes, I will kiss thy mouth, Iokanaan. I said it; did I not say it? I said it. Ah! I will kiss it now... But wherefore dost thou not look at me, Iokanaan? Thine eyes that were so terrible, so full of rage and scorn, are shut now. Wherefore are they shut? Open thine eyes! Lift up thine eyelids, Iokanaan! Wherefore dost thou not look at me? Art thou afraid of me, Iokanaan, that thou wilt not look at me?... And thy tongue, that was like a red snake darting poison, it moves no more, it speaks no words, Iokanaan, that scarlet viper that spat its venom upon me. It is strange, is it not? How is it that

the red viper stirs no longer?... Thou wouldst have none of me, Iokanaan. Thou rejectedst me. Thou didst speak evil words against me. Thy didst bear thyself toward me as to a harlot, as to a woman that is a wanton, to me, Salome, daughter of Herodias, Princess of Judæa! Well, I still live, but thou art dead, and thy head belongs to me. I can do with it what I will. I can throw it to the dogs and to the birds of the air. That which the dogs leave, the birds of the air shall devour... Ah, Iokanaan, Iokanaan, thou wert the man that I loved alone among men! All other men were hateful to me. But thou wert beautiful! Thy body was a column of ivory set upon feet of silver. It was a garden full of doves and lilies of silver. It was a tower of silver decked with shields of ivory. There was nothing in the world so white as thy body. There was nothing in the world so black as thy hair. In the whole world there was nothing so red as thy mouth. Thy voice was a censer that scattered strange perfumes, and when I looked on thee I heard a strange music. Ah! wherefore didst thou not look at me, Iokanaan? With the cloak of thine hands, and with the cloak of thy blasphemies thou didst hide thy face. Thou didst put upon thine eyes the covering of him who would see his God. Well, thou hast seen thy God, Iokanaan, but me, me, thou didst never see. If thou hadst seen me thou hadst loved me. I saw thee, and I loved thee. Oh, how I loved thee! I love thee yet, Iokanaan. I love only thee... I am athirst for thy beauty; I am hungry for thy body; and neither wine nor apples can appease my desire. What shall I do now, Iokanaan? Neither the floods nor the great waters can quench my passion. I was a princess, and thou didst scorn me. I was a virgin, and thou didst take my virginity from me. I was chaste, and thou didst fill my veins with fire... Ah! ah! wherefore didst thou not look at me? If thou hadst looked at me thou hadst loved me. Well I know that thou wouldst have loved me, and the mystery of Love is greater than the mystery of Death.

HEROD: She is monstrous, thy daughter; I tell thee she is monstrous. In truth, what she has done is a great crime. I am sure that it is a crime against some unknown God.

HERODIAS: I am well pleased with my daughter. She has done well. And I would stay here now.

HEROD: *[Rising]* Ah! There speaks my brother's wife! Come! I will not stay in this place. Come, I tell thee. Surely some terrible thing will befall. Manasseh, Issachar, Ozias, put out the torches. I will not look at things, I will not suffer things to look at me. Put out the torches! Hide the moon! Hide the stars! Let us hide ourselves in our palace, Herodias. I begin to be afraid. *[The slaves put out the torches. The stars disappear. A great cloud crosses the moon and conceals it completely. The Tetrarch begins to climb the staircase]*

THE VOICE OF SALOME: Ah! I have kissed thy mouth, Iokanaan, I have kissed thy mouth. There was a bitter taste on thy lips. Was it the taste of blood?... Nay; but perchance it was the taste of love... They say that love hath a bitter taste... But what matter? what matter? I have kissed thy mouth, Iokanaan, I have kissed thy mouth. *[A ray of moonlight falls on Salome and illumines her]*

HEROD: *[Turning round and seeing Salome]* Kill that woman! *[The soldiers rush forward and crush beneath their shields Salome, daughter of Herodias, Princess of Judæa]*

CURTAIN

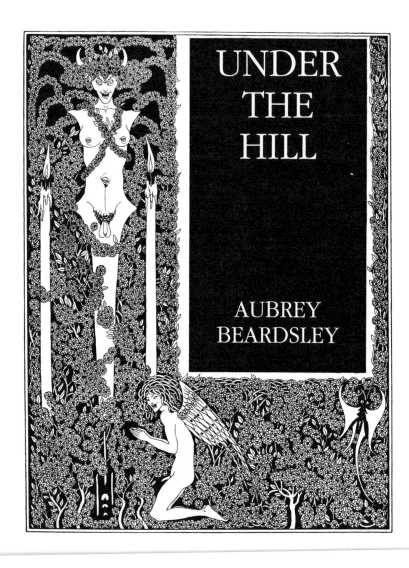

UNDER
THE
HILL

AUBREY
BEARDSLEY

UNDER THE HILL

OR THE STORY OF VENUS AND TANNHÄUSER,
IN WHICH IS SET FORTH AN EXACT ACCOUNT
OF THE MANNER OF STATE HELD BY
MADAME VENUS, GODDESS AND MERETRIX,
UNDER THE FAMOUS HORSELBERG,
AND CONTAINING THE ADVENTURES OF
TANNHÄUSER IN THAT PLACE,
HIS JOURNEYING TO ROME,
AND RETURN TO THE LOVING MOUNTAIN,
BY
AUBREY BEARDSLEY

Pictured
by
AUBREY BEARDSLEY

TO
THE MOST EMINENT AND REVERED PRINCE

GIULIO POLDO PEZZOLI

CARDINAL OF THE HOLY ROMAN CHURCH
TITULAR BISHOP OF S. MARIA IN TRASTEVERE
ARCHBISHOP OF OSTIA AND VELLETRI
NUNCIO TO THE HOLY SEE
IN
NICARAGUA AND PATAGONIA
A FATHER TO THE POOR
A REFORMER OF ECCLESIASTICAL DISCIPLINE
A PATTERN OF LEARNING
WISDOM AND HOLINESS OF LIFE
THIS BOOK IS DEDICATED WITH DUE REVERENCE
BY HIS HUMBLE SERVITOR
A SCRIVENER AND LIMNER OF WORDLY THINGS
WHO MADE THIS BOOK

AUBREY BEARDSLEY

MOST EMINENT PRINCE,

I KNOW NOT BY WHAT MISCHANCE THE WRITING OF
EPISTLES DEDICATORY HAS FALLEN INTO DISUSE,
WHETHER THROUGH THE VANITY OF AUTHORS OR THE
HUMILITY OF PATRONS. BUT THE PRACTICE SEEMS TO ME
SO VERY BEAUTIFUL AND BECOMING THAT I HAVE
VENTURED TO MAKE AN ESSAY IN THE MODEST ART,
AND LAY WITH FORMALITIES MY FIRST BOOK AT YOUR
FEET. I HAVE, IT MUST BE CONFESSED, MANY FEARS LEST
I SHALL BE ARRAIGNED OF PRESUMPTION IN CHOOSING
SO EXALTED A NAME AS YOUR OWN TO PLACE AT THE
BEGINNING OF THIS HISTORY; BUT I HOPE THAT SUCH
A CENSURE WILL NOT BE TOO LIGHTLY PASSED UPON
ME, FOR IF I AM GUILTY IT IS BUT OF A MOST NATURAL
PRIDE THAT THE ACCIDENTS OF MY LIFE SHOULD ALLOW
ME TO SAIL THE LITTLE PINNACE OF MY WIT UNDER
YOUR PROTECTION.

BUT THOUGH I CAN CLEAR MYSELF OF SUCH A CHARGE,
I AM STILL MINDED TO USE THE TONGUE OF APOLOGY,
FOR WITH WHAT FACE CAN I OFFER YOU A BOOK
TREATING OF SO VAIN AND FANTASTICAL A THING AS
LOVE? I KNOW THAT IN THE JUDGMENT OF MANY THE
AMOROUS PASSION IS ACCOUNTED A SHAMEFUL THING
AND RIDICULOUS; INDEED IT MUST BE CONFESSED THAT
MORE BLUSHES HAVE RISEN FOR LOVE'S SAKE THAN FOR

ANY OTHER CAUSE, AND THAT LOVERS ARE AN ETERNAL LAUGHING-STOCK. STILL, AS THE BOOK WILL BE FOUND TO CONTAIN MATTER OF DEEPER IMPORT THAN MERE VENERY, INASMUCH AS IT TREATS OF THE GREAT CONTRITION OF ITS CHIEFEST CHARACTER, AND OF CANONICAL THINGS IN CERTAIN PAGES, I AM NOT WITHOUT HOPES THAT YOUR EMINENCE WILL PARDON MY WRITING OF THE HILL OF VENUS, FOR WHICH EXTRAVAGANCE LET MY YOUTH EXCUSE ME.

THEN I MUST CRAVE YOUR FORGIVENESS FOR ADDRESSING YOU IN A LANGUAGE OTHER THAN THE ROMAN, BUT MY SMALL FREEDOM IN LATINITY FORBIDS ME TO WANDER BEYOND THE IDIOM OF MY VERNA-CULAR. I WOULD NOT FOR THE WORLD THAT YOUR DELICATE SOUTHERN EAR SHOULD BE OFFENDED BY A BARBAROUS ASSAULT OF RUDE AND GOTHIC WORDS; BUT METHINKS NO LANGUAGE IS RUDE THAT CAN BOAST POLITE WRITERS, AND NOT A FEW SUCH HAVE FLOURISHED IN THIS COUNTRY IN TIMES PAST, BRINGING OUR COMMON SPEECH TO VERY GREAT PERFECTION. IN THE PRESENT AGE, ALAS! OUR PENS ARE RAVISHED BY UNLETTERED AUTHORS AND UNMANNERED CRITICS, THAT MAKE A HAVOC RATHER THAN A BUILDING, A WILDERNESS RATHER THAN A GARDEN. BUT, ALACK! WHAT BOOTS IT TO DROP TEARS UPON THE PRETERIT?

IT IS NOT OF OUR OWN SHORTCOMINGS THOUGH, BUT OF YOUR NOW GREAT MERITS THAT I SHOULD SPEAK, ELSE I SHOULD BE FORGETFUL OF THE DUTIES I HAVE DRAWN UPON MYSELF IN ELECTING TO ADDRESS YOU IN A DEDICATION. IT IS OF YOUR NOBLE VIRTUES (THOUGH ALL THE WORLD KNOW OF 'EM), YOUR TASTE AND WIT, YOUR CARE FOR LETTERS, AND VERY REAL REGARD FOR

THE ARTS THAT I MUST BE THE PROCLAIMER.

THOUGH IT BE TRUE THAT ALL MEN HAVE SUFFICIENT
WIT TO PASS A JUDGMENT ON THIS OR THAT, AND NOT
A FEW SUFFICIENT IMPUDENCE TO PRINT THE SAME (THE
LAST BEING COMMONLY ACCOUNTED CRITICS), I HAVE
EVER HELD THAT THE CRITICAL FACULTY IS MORE RARE
THAN THE INVENTIVE. IT IS A FACULTY YOUR EMINENCE
POSSESSES IN SO GREAT A DEGREE THAT YOUR PRAISE
OR BLAME IS SOMETHING ORACULAR, YOUR UTTERANCE
INFALLIBLE AS GREAT GENIUS OR AS A BEAUTIFUL
WOMAN. YOUR MIND, I KNOW, REJOICING IN FINE
DISTINCTIONS AND SUBTLE PROCEDURES OF THOUGHT,
BEAUTIFULLY DISCURSIVE RATHER THAN HASTILY
CONTRIBUTED, HAS FOUND IN CRITICISM ITS HAPPIEST
EXERCISE. IT IS A PITY THAT SO PERFECT A MECENAS
SHOULD HAVE NO HORACE TO BEFRIEND, NO GEORGICS
TO ACCEPT; FOR THE OFFICES AND FUNCTION OF
PATRON OR CRITIC MUST OF NECESSITY BE LESSENED IN
AN AGE OF LITTLE MEN AND LITTLE WORK. IN TIMES
PAST IT WAS NOTHING DEROGATORY FOR GREAT
PRINCES AND MEN OF STATE TO EXTEND THEIR LOVES
AND FAVOUR TO POETS, FOR THEREBY THEY RECEIVED
AS MUCH HONOUR AS THEY CONFERRED. DID NOT
PRINCE FESTUS WITH PRIDE TAKE THE MASTERWORK OF
JULIAN INTO HIS PROTECTION, AND WAS NOT THE ÆNEIS
A PRETTY THING TO OFFER CÆSAR?

LEARNING WITHOUT APPRECIATION IS A THING OF
NAUGHT, BUT KNOW NOT WHICH IS GREATEST IN YOU
— YOUR LOVE OF THE ARTS, OR YOUR KNOWLEDGE OF
'EM. WHAT WONDER THEN THAT I AM STUDIOUS TO
PLEASE YOU, AND DESIROUS OF YOUR PROTECTION?
HOW DEEPLY THANKFUL I AM FOR YOUR PAST

AFFECTIONS YOU KNOW WELL, YOUR GREAT KINDNESS AND LIBERALITY HAVING FAR OUTGONE MY SLIGHT MERITS AND SMALL ACCOMPLISHMENTS THAT SEEMED SCARCE TO WARRANT ANY FAVOUR. ALAS! 'TIS A SLIGHT OFFERING I MAKE YOU NOW, BUT IF AFTER GLANCING INTO ITS PACES (SAY OF AN EVENING UPON YOUR TERRACE) YOU SHOULD DEEM IT WORTHY OF THE REMOTEST PLACE IN YOUR PRINCELY LIBRARY, THE KNOWLEDGE THAT IT RESTED THERE WOULD BE REWARD SUFFICIENT FOR MY LABOURS, AND A CROWNING HAPPINESS TO MY PLEASURE IN THE WRITING OF THIS SLENDER BOOK.

THE HUMBLE AND OBEDIENT SERVANT OF YOUR EMINENCE,

AUBREY BEARDSLEY.

CHAPTER I

How the Chevalier Tannhäuser
entered into the Hill of Venus

The Chevalier Tannhäuser, having lighted off his horse, stood doubtfully for a moment beneath the sombre gateway of the mysterious Hill, troubled with an exquisite fear lest a day's travel should have too cruelly undone the laboured niceness of his dress. His hand, slim and gracious as La Marquise du Deffand's in the drawing by Carmontelle, played nervously about the gold hair that fell upon his shoulders like a finely-curled peruke, and from point to point of a precise toilet the fingers wandered, quelling the little mutinies of cravat and ruffle.

It was taper-time; when the tired earth puts on its cloak of mists and shadows, when the enchanted woods are stirred with light footfalls and slender voices of the fairies, when all the air is full of delicate influences, and even the beaux, seated at their dressing-tables, dream a little.

A delicious moment, thought Tannhäuser, to slip into exile.

The place where he stood waved drowsily with strange flowers, heavy with perfume, dripping with odours. Gloomy and nameless weeds not to be found in Mentzelius. Huge moths, so richly winged they must have banqueted upon tapestries and royal stuffs, slept on the pillars that flanked either side of the gateway, and the eyes of all the moths remained open and were burning and bursting with a mesh of veins. The pillars were fashioned in some pale stone and rose up like hymns in the praise of pleasure, for from cap to base, each one was carved with loving sculptures, showing such a cunning invention and such a curious knowledge, that Tannhäuser lingered not a little in reviewing them. They surpassed all that Japan has ever pictured from her *maisons vertes*, all that was ever painted in the cool bathrooms of Cardinal La Motte, and even outdid the astonishing illustrations to Jones's "Nursery Numbers".

"A pretty portal," murmured the Chevalier, correcting his sash.

As he spoke, a faint sound of singing was breathed out from the mountain, faint music as strange and distant as sea-legends that are heard in shells.

"The Vespers of Venus, I take it," said Tannhäuser, and struck a few chords of accompaniment, ever so lightly, upon his little lute. Softly across the spell-bound threshold the song floated and wreathed itself about the subtle columns, till the moths were touched with passion and moved quaintly in their sleep. One of them was awakened by the intenser notes of the Chevalier's lute-strings, and fluttered into the cave. Tannhäuser felt it was his cue for entry.

"Adieu," he exclaimed with an inclusive gesture, "and goodbye, Madonna," as the cold circle of the moon began to show, beautiful and full of enchantments. There was a shadow of sentiment in his voice as he spoke the words.

"Would to heaven," he sighed, "I might receive the assurance of a looking-glass before I make my debut! However, as she is a goddess, I doubt not her eyes are a little sated with perfection, and may not be displeased to see it crowned with a tiny fault."

A wild rose had caught upon the trimmings of his ruff, and in the first flush of displeasure he would have struck it brusquely away, and most severely punished the offending flower. But the ruffled mood lasted only a moment, for there was something so deliciously incongruous in the hardy petal's invasion of so delicate a thing, that Tannhäuser withheld the finger of resentment and vowed that the wild rose should stay where it had clung — a passport, as it were, from the upper to the lower world.

"The very excess and violence of the fault," he said, "will be its excuse;" and, undoing a tangle in the tassel of his stick, stepped into the shadowy corridor that ran into the bosom of the wan hill — stepped with the admirable aplomb and unwrinkled suavity of Don Juan.

CHAPTER II

*Of the manner in which Venus
was coiffed and prepared for supper*

Before a toilet that shone like the altar of Notre Dame des
Victoires, Venus was seated in a little dressing-gown of black
and heliotrope. The coiffeur Cosmé was caring for her
scented chevelure, and with tiny silver tongs, warm from the
caresses of the flame, made delicious intelligent curls that fell
as lightly as a breath about her forehead and over her
eyebrows, and clustered like tendrils round her neck. Her
three favourite girls, Pappelarde, Blanchemains and Loreyne,
waited immediately upon her with perfume and powder in
delicate flacons and frail cassolettes, and held in porcelain jars
the ravishing paints prepared by Châteline for those cheeks
and lips that had grown a little pale with anguish of exile. Her
three favourite boys, Claude, Clair and Sarrasine, stood
amorously about with salver, fan and napkin. Millamant held
a slight tray of slippers, Minette some tender gloves, La
Popelinière — mistress of the robes — was ready with a frock
of yellow and white, La Zambinella bore the jewels, Florizel
some flowers, Amadour a box of various pins, and Vadius a
box of sweets. Her doves, ever in attendance, walked about
the room that was panelled with the gallant paintings of Jean

Baptiste Dorat, and some dwarfs and doubtful creatures sat here and there lolling out their tongues, pinching each other, and behaving oddly enough. Sometimes Venus gave them little smiles.

As the toilet was in progress, Mrs. Marsuple, the fat manicure and fardeuse, strode in and seated herself by the side of the dressing-table, greeting Venus with an intimate nod. She wore a gown of white watered silk with gold lace trimmings, and a velvet necklet of false vermilion. Her hair hung in bandeaux over her ears, passing into a huge chignon at the back of her head, and the hat, wide-brimmed and hung with a valiance of pink muslin, was floral with red roses.

Mrs. Marsuple's voice was full of salacious unction; she had terrible little gestures with the hands, strange movements with the shoulders, a short respiration that made surprising wrinkles in her bodice, a corrupt skin, large horny eyes, a parrot's nose, a small loose mouth, great flaccid cheeks, and chin after chin. She was a wise person, and Venus loved her more than any of her servants, and had a hundred pet names for her, such as Dear Toad, Pretty Poll, Cock Robin, Dearest Lip, Touchstone, Little Cough Drop, Bijou, Buttons, Dear Heart, Dick-Dock, Mrs. Manly, Little Nipper, Cochon-de-lait, Naughty-naughty, Blessed Thing, and Trump. The talk that passed between Mrs. Marsuple and her mistress was of that excellent kind that passes between old friends, a perfect understanding giving to scraps of phrases their full meaning, and to the merest reference a point. Naturally Tannhäuser the newcomer was discussed a little. Venus had not seen him yet, and asked a score of questions on his account that were delightfully to the point. Mrs. Marsuple told the story of his arrival, his curious wandering in the gardens, and calm satisfaction with all he saw there, his impromptu affection for a slender girl upon the first terrace, of the crowd of frocks that gathered round and pelted him with roses, of the graceful way he defended himself with his mask, and of the queer reverence he made to the God of all gardens, kissing that deity with a pilgrim's devotion. Just then Tannhäuser was at the baths, and was creating a favourable impression.

The report and the coiffing were completed at the same moment. "Cosmé," said Venus, "you have been quite sweet and quite brilliant, you have surpassed yourself tonight."

"Madam flatters me," replied the antique old thing, with a girlish giggle under his black satin mask. "Gad, Madam; sometimes I believe I have no talent in the world, but tonight I must confess to a touch of the vain mood."

It would pain me horribly to tell you about the painting of her face; suffice it that the sorrowful work was accomplished; frankly, magnificently, and without a shadow of deception.

Venus slipped away the dressing-gown, and rose before the mirror in a flutter of frilled things. She was adorably tall and slender. Her neck and shoulders were wonderfully drawn, and the little malicious breasts were full of the irritation of loveliness that can never be entirely comprehended, or ever enjoyed to the utmost. Her arms and hands were loosely, but delicately articulated, and her legs were divinely long. From the hip to the knee, twenty-two inches; from the knee to the heel, twenty-two inches, as befitted a goddess.

I should like to speak more particularly about her, for generalities are not of the slightest service in a description. But I am afraid that an enforced silence here and there would leave such numerous gaps in the picture that it had better not be begun at all than left unfinished. Those who have seen Venus only in the Vatican, in the Louvre, in the Uffizi, or in the British Museum, can have no idea of how very beautiful and sweet she looked. Not at all like the lady in "Lemprière".

Mrs. Marsuple grew quite lyrical over the dear little

person, and pecked at her arms with kisses.

"Dear Tongue, you must really behave yourself," said Venus, and called Millamant to bring her the slippers.

The tray was freighted with the most exquisite and shapely pantoufles, sufficient to make Cluny a place of naught. There were shoes of grey and black and brown suède, of white silk and rose satin, and velvet and sarcenet; there were some of sea-green sewn with cherry blossoms, some of red with willow branches, and some of grey with bright-winged birds. There were heels of silver, of ivory, and of gilt; there were buckles of very precious stones set in most strange and esoteric devices; there were ribbons tied and twisted into cunning forms; there were buttons so beautiful that the buttonholes might have no pleasure till they closed upon them; there were soles of delicate leathers scented with maréchale, and linings of soft stuffs scented with the juice of July flowers. But Venus, finding none of them to her mind, called for a discarded pair of blood-red maroquin, diapered with pearls. They looked very distinguished over her white silk stockings. As the tray was being carried away, the capricious Florizel snatched as usual a slipper from it, and fitted the foot over his penis, and made the necessary movements. That was Florizel's little caprice. Meantime, La Popelinière stepped forward with the frock.

"I shan't wear one tonight," said Venus. Then she slipped on her gloves.

When the toilet was at an end all her doves clustered round her feet loving to *frôler* her ankles with their plumes, and the dwarfs clapped their hands, and put their fingers between their lips and whistled. Never before had Venus been so radiant and compelling. Spiridion, in the corner, looked up from his game of Spellicans and trembled. Claude and Clair, pale with pleasure, stroked and touched her with their delicate hands, and wrinkled her stockings with their nervous lips, and smoothed them with their thin fingers; and Sarrasine undid her garters and kissed them inside and put them on again, pressing her thighs with his mouth. The dwarfs grew very daring, I can tell you. There was almost a *mêlée*. They illustrated pages 72 and 73 of Delvau's Dictionary.

In the middle of it all, Pranzmungel announced that supper was ready upon the fifth terrace. "Ah!" cried Venus, "I'm famished!"

CHAPTER III

How Venus supped;
and thereafter was mightily amused
by the curious pranks of her entourage

She was quite delighted with Tannhäuser, and, of course, he sat next her at supper.

The terrace, made beautiful with a thousand vain and fantastical things, and set with a hundred tables and four hundred couches, presented a truly splendid appearance. In the middle was a huge bronze fountain with three basins. From the first rose a many-breasted dragon and four little loves mounted upon swans, and each love was furnished with a bow and arrow. Two of them that faced the monster seemed to recoil in fear, two that were behind made bold enough to aim their shafts at him. From the verge of the second sprang a circle of slim golden columns that supported silver doves with tails and wings spread out. The third, held by a group of grotesquely attenuated satyrs, was centred with a thin pipe hung with masks and roses and capped with children's heads.

From the mouths of the dragon and the loves, from the swans' eyes, from the breasts of the doves, from the satyrs' horns and lips, from the masks at many points, and from the children's curls, the water played profusely, cutting strange arabesques and subtle figures.

The terrace was lit entirely by candles. There were four thousand of them, not numbering those upon the tables. The candlesticks were of a countless variety, and smiled with moulded *cochonneries.* Some were twenty feet high, and bore single candles that flared like fragrant torches over the feast, and guttered till the wax stood round the tops in tall lances. Some, hung with dainty petticoats of shining lustres, had a whole bevy of tapers upon them devised in circles, in pyramids, in squares, in cuneiforms, in single lines regimentally and in crescents.

Then on quaint pedestals and Terminal Gods and gracious pilasters of every sort, were shell-like vases of excessive fruits and flowers that hung about and burst over the edges and could never be restrained. The orange-trees and myrtles, looped with vermilion sashes, stood in frail porcelain pots, and the rose-trees were wound and twisted with superb invention over trellis and standard. Upon one side of the terrace a long gilded stage for the comedians was curtained off with Pagonian tapestries, and in front of it the music-stands were placed.

The tables arranged between the fountain and the flight of steps to the sixth terrace were all circular, covered with white damask, and strewn with irises, roses, kingcups, colombines, daffodils, carnations and lilies; and the couches, high with soft cushions and spread with more stuffs than could be named, had fans thrown upon them, and little amorous surprise packets.

Beyond the escalier stretched the gardens, which were designed so elaborately and with so much splendour that the architect of the Fêtes d'Armailhacq could have found in them no matter for cavil, and the still lakes strewn with profuse barges full of gay flowers and wax marionettes, the alleys of tall trees, the arcades and cascades, the pavilions, the grottoes and the garden-gods — all took a strange tinge of revelry from the glare of the light that fell upon them from the feast.

The frockless Venus and Tannhäuser, with Mrs. Marsuple and Claude and Clair, and Farcy, the chief comedian, sat at the same table. Tannhäuser, who had doffed his travelling suit, wore long black silk stockings, a pair of pretty garters, a very elegant ruffled shirt, slippers and a wonderful dressing-gown; Claude and Clair wore nothing at all, delicious privilege of immaturity; and Farey was in ordinary evening clothes. As for the rest of the company, it boasted some very noticeable dresses, and whole tables of quite delightful coiffures. There were spotted veils that seemed to stain the skin with some exquisite and august disease, fans with eye-slits in them, through which the bearers peeped and peered; fans painted with figures and covered with the sonnets of Sporion and the short stories of Scaramouch; and fans of big, living moths stuck upon mounts of silver sticks. There were masks of green velvet that make the face look trebly powdered; masks of the heads of birds, of apes, of serpents, of dolphins, of men and women, of little embryons and of cats; masks like the faces of gods; masks of coloured glass, and masks of thin talc and of india-rubber. There were wigs of black and scarlet wools, of peacocks' feathers, of gold and silver threads, of swansdown, of the tendrils of the vine, and of human hair; huge collars of stiff muslin rising high above the head; whole dresses of ostrich feathers curling inwards; tunics of panthers' skins that looked beautiful over pink tights; capotes of crimson satin trimmed with the wings of owls; sleeves cut into the shapes of apocryphal animals; drawers flounced down to the ankles, and flecked with tiny, red roses; stockings clocked with *fêtes galantes,* and curious designs; and petticoats cut like artificial flowers. Some of the women had put on delightful little moustaches dyed in purples and bright greens, twisted and waxed with absolute skill; and some wore great white beards, after the manner of Saint Wilgeforte. Then Dorat had painted extraordinary grotesques and vignettes over their bodies, here and there. Upon a cheek, an old man scratching his horned head; upon a forehead, an old woman teased by an impudent amour; upon a shoulder, an amorous singerie; round a breast, a circlet of satyrs; about a wrist, a wreath of pale, unconscious babes; upon an elbow a bouquet of spring flowers; across a back, some surprising scenes of adventure; at the corners of a mouth, tiny, red spots; and upon a neck, a flight of birds, a caged parrot, a branch of fruit, a butterfly, a spider, a drunken dwarf, or, simply, some initials. But most wonderful of all were the black silhouettes painted upon the legs, and which showed through a white silk stocking like a sumptuous bruise.

The supper provided by the ingenious Rambouillet was quite beyond parallel. Never had he created a more exquisite menu. The *consommé impromptu* alone would have been sufficient to establish the immortal reputation of any chef. What, then, can I say of the *Dorade bouillie sauce maréchale*, the *ragoût aux langues de carpes*, the *ramereaux à la charnière*, the *ciboulette de gibier à l'espagnole*, the *paté de cuisses d'oie aux pois de Monsalvie*, the *queues d'agneau au clair de lune*, the *artichauts à la grecque*, the *charlotte de pommes à la Lucy Waters*, the *bombes à la marée*, and the *glaces aux rayons d'or*? A veritable *tour de cuisine* that surpassed even the famous little suppers given by the Marquis de Réchale at Passy, and which the Abbé Mirliton pronounced "impeccable, and too good to be eaten."

Ah! Pierre Antoine Berquin de Rambouillet; you are worthy of your divine mistress!

Mere hunger quickly gave place to those finer instincts of the pure gourmet, and the strange wines, cooled in buckets of snow, unloosed all the *décolleté* spirits of astonishing conversation and atrocious laughter.

CHAPTER IV

*How the court of Venus
behaved strangely at her supper*

As the courses advanced, the conversation grew bustling and
more personal. Pulex and Cyril, and Marisca and Cathelin,
opened a fire of raillery. The infidelities of Cerise, the
difficulties of Brancas, Sarmean's caprices that morning in the
lily garden, Thorillière's declining strength, Astarte's affection
for Roseola, Felix's impossible member, Cathelin's passion for
Sulpilia's poodle, Sola's passion for herself, the nasty bite that
Marisca gave Chloe, the *epilatière* of Pulex, Cyril's diseases,
Butor's illness, Maryx's tiny cemetery, Lesbia's profound fourth
letter, and a thousand amatory follies of the day were
discussed.

From harsh and shrill and clamant, the voices grew
blurred and inarticulate. Bad sentences were helped out by
worse gestures, and at one table Scabius expressed himself
like the famous old knight in the first part of the "Soldier's
Fortune" of Otway. Bassalissa and Lysistrata tried to
pronounce each other's names, and became very affectionate
in the attempt; and Tala, the tragedian, robed in roomy
purple, and wearing plume and buskin, rose to his feet, and,
with swaying gestures, began to recite one of his favourite

parts. He got no further than the first line, but repeated it again and again, with fresh accents and intonations each time, and was only silenced by the approach of the asparagus that was being served by satyrs dressed in white. Clitor and Sodon had a violent struggle over the beautiful Pella, and nearly upset a chandelier. Sophie became very intimate with an empty champagne bottle, swore it had made her *enceinte*, and ended by having a mock *accouchement* on the top of the table; and Belamour pretended to be a dog, and pranced from couch to couch on all fours, biting and barking and licking. Mellefont crept about dropping love philtres into glasses. Juventus and Ruelia stripped and put on each other's things, Spelto offered a prize for whoever should come first, and Spelto won it! Tannhäuser, just a little *grisé*, lay down on the cushions and let Julia do whatever she liked.

I wish I could be allowed to tell you what occurred round table fifteen, just at this moment. It would amuse you very much, and would give you a capital idea of the habits of Venus' retinue. Indeed, for deplorable reasons, by far the greater part of what was said and done at this supper must remain unrecorded and even unsuggested.

Venus allowed most of the dishes to pass untasted, she was so engaged with the beauty of Tannhäuser. She laid her head many times on his robe, kissing him passionately; and his skin at once firm and yielding, seemed to those exquisite little teeth of hers, the most incomparable pasture. Her upper lip curled and trembled with excitement, showing the gums. Tannhäuser, on his side, was no less devoted. He adored her all over and all the things she had on, and buried his face in the folds and flounces of her linen, and ravished away a score of frills in his excess. He found her exasperating, and crushed her in his arms, and slaked his parched lips at her mouth. He caressed her eyelids softly with his finger tips, and pushed aside the curls from her forehead, and did a thousand gracious things, tuning her body as a violinist tunes his instrument before playing upon it.

Mrs. Marsuple snorted like an old warhorse at the sniff of powder, and tickled Tannhäuser and Venus by turns, and slipped her tongue down their throats, and refused to be quiet at all until she had had a mouthful of the Chevalier. Claude, seizing his chance, dived under the table and came up on the other side just under Venus' couch, and before she could say "One!" he was taking his coffee *"aux deux colonnes"*. Clair was furious at his friend's success, and sulked for the rest of the evening.

CHAPTER V

*Of the ballet danced
by the servants of Venus*

I

After the fruits and fresh wines had been brought in by a troop of woodland creatures, decked with green leaves and all sorts of spring flowers, the candles in the orchestra were lit, and in another moment the musicians bustled into their places. The wonderful Titurel de Schentefleur was the *chef d'orchestre*, and the most insidious of conductors. His baton dived into a phrase and brought out the most magical and magnificent things, and seemed rather to play every instrument than to lead it. He could add grace even to Scarlatti and a wonder to Beethoven. A delicate, thin, little man with thick lips and a *nez retroussé*, with long black hair and curled moustache, in the manner of Molière. What were his amatory tastes, no one in the Venusberg could tell. He generally passed for a virgin, and Cathos had nicknamed him "The Solitaire".

Tonight he appeared in a court suit of white silk, brilliant with decorations. His hair was curled in resplendent ringlets that trembled like springs at the merest gesture of his arm, and in his ears swung the diamonds given him by Venus.

The orchestra was, as usual, in its uniform of red vest and breeches trimmed with gold lace, white stockings and red shoes. Titurel had written a ballet for the evening *divertissement*, founded upon De Bergerac's comedy of "Les Bacchanales de Sporion", in which the action and dances were designed by him as well as the music.

The curtain rose upon a scene of rare beauty, a remote Arcadian valley, a delicious scrap of Tempe, gracious with cool woods and watered with a little river. It was early morning and the re-arisen sun, like the prince in the Sleeping Beauty, woke all the earth with his lips.

In that golden embrace the night dews were caught up and made splendid, the trees were awakened from their obscure dreams, the slumber of the birds was broken, and all the flowers of the valley rejoiced, forgetting their fear of the darkness.

Suddenly to the music of pipe and horn a troop of satyrs stepped out from the recesses of the woods bearing in their hands nuts and green boughs and flowers and roots, and whatsoever the forest yielded, to heap upon the altar of the mysterious Pan that stood in the middle of the stage; and from the hills came down the shepherds and shepherdesses leading their flocks and carrying garlands upon their crooks. Then a rustic priest, white robed and venerable, came slowly across the valley followed by a choir of radiant children. The scene was admirably stage-managed and nothing could have been more varied yet harmonious than this Arcadian group. The service was quaint and simple, but with sufficient ritual to give the *corps de ballet* an opportunity of showing its dainty skill. The dancing of the satyrs was received with huge favour, and when the priest raised his hand in final blessing, the whole troop of worshippers made such an intricate and elegant exit, that it was generally agreed that Titurel had never before shown so fine an invention.

Scarcely had the stage been empty for a moment, when Sporion entered, followed by a brilliant rout of dandies and smart women. Sporion was a tall, slim, depraved young man with a slight stoop, a troubled walk, an oval impassible face with its olive skin drawn tightly over the bone, strong, scarlet lips, long Japanese eyes, and a great gilt toupet. Round his shoulders hung a high-collared satin cape of salmon pink with long black ribands untied and floating about his body. His coat of sea-green spotted muslin was caught in at the waist by a scarlet sash with scalloped edges and frilled out over the hips for about six inches. His trousers, loose and wrinkled, reached to the end of the calf, and were brocaded down the sides and ruched magnificently at the ankles. The stockings were of white kid with stalls for the toes, and had delicate red sandals strapped over them. But his little hands, peeping out from their frills, seemed quite the most insinuating things, such supple fingers tapering to the point with tiny nails stained pink, such unquenchable palms lined and mounted like Lord Fanny's in "Love At All Hazards", and such blue veined hairless backs! In his left hand he carried a small lace handkerchief broidered with a coronet.

As for his friends and followers, they made the most superb and insolent crowd imaginable, but to catalogue the clothes they had on would require a chapter as long as the famous tenth in Pénillière's "History Of Underlinen". On the whole they looked a very distinguished chorus.

Sporion stepped forward and explained with swift and various gesture that he and his friends were tired of the amusements, wearied with the poor pleasure offered by the civil world, and had invaded the Arcadian valley hoping to experience a new *frisson* in the destruction of some shepherd's or some satyr's *naïveté*, and the infusion of their venom among the dwellers of the woods.

The chorus assented with languid but expressive movements.

Curious and not a little frightened at the arrival of the worldly company, the sylvans began to peep nervously at those subtle souls through the branches of the trees, and one or two fauns and a shepherd or so crept out warily. Sporion and all the ladies and gentlemen made enticing sounds and invited the rustic creatures with all the grace in the world to come and join them. By little batches they came, lured by the strange looks, by the scents and the drugs, and by the brilliant clothes, and some ventured quite near, timorously fingering the delicious textures of the stuffs. Then Sporion and each of his friends took a satyr or a shepherdess or something by the hand and made the preliminary steps of a courtly measure, for which the most admirable combinations had been invented and the most charming music written. The pastoral folk were entirely bewildered when they saw such restrained and graceful movements, and made the most grotesque and futile efforts to imitate them. *Dio mio*, a pretty sight! A charming effect, too, was obtained by the intermixture of stockinged calf and hairy leg, of rich brocaded bodice and plain blouse, of tortured head-dress and loose untutored locks.

When the dance was ended the servants of Sporion brought on champagne, and with many pirouettes poured it magnificently into slender glasses, and tripped about plying those Arcadian mouths that had never before tasted such a royal drink.

II

'Twas not long before the invaders began to enjoy the first fruits of their expedition, plucking them in the most seductive manner with their smooth fingers, and feasting lip and tongue and tooth, whilst the shepherds and satyrs and shepherdesses fairly gasped under the new joys, for the pleasure they experienced was almost too keen for their simple and untilled natures. Sporion and the rest of the rips and ladies tingled with excitement and frolicked like young lambs in a fresh meadow. Again and again the wine was danced round, and the valley grew as busy as a market day. Attracted by the noise and the merrymaking, all those sweet infants I told you of, skipped suddenly on to the stage, and began clapping their hands and laughing immoderately at the passion and disorder and commotion, and mimicking the nervous staccato movements they saw in their pretty childish way.

In a flash Sporion disentangled himself and sprang to his feet, gesticulating as if he would say, "Ah, the little dears!" "Ah, the rorty little things!" "Ah, the little ducks!" for he was so fond of children. Scarcely had he caught one by the thigh than a quick rush was made by everybody for the succulent limbs; and how they tousled them and mousled them! The children cried out, I can tell you. Of course there were not enough for everybody, so some had to share, and some had simply to go on with what they were doing before.

I must not, by the way, forget to mention the independent attitude taken by six or seven of the party, who sat and stood about with half-closed eyes, inflated nostrils, clenched teeth, and painful, parted lips, behaving like the Due de Broglie when he watched the amours of the Régent d'Orléans.

Now as Sporion and his friends began to grow tired and exhausted with the new debauch, they cared no longer to take the initiative, but, relaxing every muscle, abandoned themselves to passive joys, yielding utterly to the ardent embraces of the intoxicated satyrs, who waxed fast and furious, and seemed as if they would never come to the end of their strength. Full of the new tricks they had learnt that morning, they played them passionately and roughly, making havoc of the cultured flesh, and tearing the splendid frocks and dresses into ribands. Duchesses and Maréchales, Marquises and Princesses, Dukes and Marshals, Marquesses and Princes, were ravished and stretched and rumpled and crushed beneath the interminable vigour and hairy breasts of the inflamed woodlanders. They bit at the white thighs and nozzled wildly in the crevices. They sat astride the women's chests and consummated frantically with their bosoms; they caught their prey by the hips and held it over their heads, irrumating with prodigious gusto. It was the triumph of the valley.

High up in the heavens the sun had mounted and filled all the air with generous warmth, whilst shadows grew shorter and sharper. Little light-winged papillons flitted across the stage, the bees made music on their flowery way, the birds were gay and kept up a jargoning and refraining, the lambs were bleating upon the hillside, and the orchestra kept playing, playing the uncanny tunes of Titurel.

CHAPTER VI

*Of the amourous encounter which took place
between Venus and Tannhäuser*

Venus and Tannhäuser had retired to the exquisite little
boudoir or pavilion Le Con had designed for the queen on
the first terrace, and which commanded the most delicious
view of the parks and gardens. It was a sweet little place, all
silk curtains and soft cushions. There were eight sides to it,
bright with mirrors and candelabra, and rich with pictured
panels, and the ceiling, dome-shaped and some thirty feet
above the head, shone obscurely with gilt mouldings through
the warm haze of candle light below. Tiny wax statuettes
dressed theatrically and smiling with plump cheeks, quaint
magots that looked as cruel as foreign gods, gilded
monticules, pale celadon vases, clocks that said nothing, ivory
boxes full of secrets, china figurines playing whole scenes of
plays, and a world of strange preciousness crowded the
curious cabinets that stood against the walls. On one side of
the room there were six perfect little card tables, with quite
the daintiest and most elegant chairs set primly round them;
so, after all, there may be some truth in that line of Mr.
Theodore Watts—

"I played at picquet with the Queen of Love."

Nothing in the pavilion was more beautiful than the folding screens painted by De La Pine, with Claudian landscapes — the sort of things that fairly make one melt, things one can lie and look at for hours together, and forget the country can ever be dull and tiresome. There were four of them, delicate walls that hem in an amour so cosily, and make room within room.

The place was scented with huge branches of red roses, and with a faint amatory perfume breathed out from the couches and cushions — a perfume Châteline distilled in secret and called *L'Eau Lavante*.

Cosmé's precise curls and artful waves had been finally disarranged at supper, and strayed ringlets of the black hair fell loosely over Venus' soft, delicious, tired, swollen eyelids. Her frail chemise and dear little drawers were torn and moist, and clung transparently about her, and all her body was nervous and responsive. Her closed thighs seemed like a vast replica of the little bijou she had between them; the beautiful *tétons du derrière* were firm as a plump virgin's cheek, and promised a joy as profound as the mystery of the Rue Vendôme, and the minor chevelure, just profuse enough, curled as prettily as the hair upon a cherub's head.

Tannhäuser, pale and speechless with excitement, passed his gem-girt fingers brutally over the divine limbs, tearing away smock and pantalon and stocking, and then, stripping himself of his own few things, fell upon the splendid lady with a deep-drawn breath!

It is, I know, the custom of all romancers to paint heroes who can give a lady proof of their valiance at least twenty times a night. Now Tannhäuser had no such Gargantuan felicity, and was rather relieved when, an hour later, Mrs. Marsuple and Doricourt and some others burst drunkenly into the room and claimed Venus for themselves. The pavilion soon filled with a noisy crowd that could scarcely keep its feet. Several of the actors were there, and Lesfesses, who had played Sporion so brilliantly, and was still in his make-up, paid tremendous attention to Tannhäuser. But the Chevalier found him quite uninteresting off the stage, and rose and crossed the room to where Venus and the manicure were seated.

"How tired the poor baby looks," said Mrs. Marsuple. "Shall I put him in his little cot?"

"Well, if he's as sleepy as I am," yawned Venus, "you can't do better."

Mrs. Marsuple lifted her mistress off the pillows, and carried her in her arms in a nice, motherly way.

"Come along, children," said the fat old thing, "come along; it's time you were both in bed."

CHAPTER VII

How Tannhäuser awakened and took his
morning ablutions in the Venusberg

It is always delightful to wake up in a new bedroom. The fresh wallpaper, the strange pictures, the positions of doors and windows, imperfectly grasped the night before, are revealed with all the charm of surprise when we open our eyes the next morning. ،

It was about eight o'clock when Tannhäuser awoke, stretched himself deliciously in his great plumed four-post bed, murmured "What a pretty room!" and freshened the frilled silk pillows behind him. Through the slim parting of the long flowered window curtains, he caught a peep of the sun-lit lawns outside, the silver fountains, the bright flowers, the gardeners at work, and beneath the shady trees some early breakfasters, dressed for a day's hunting in the distant wooded valleys.

"How sweet it all is," exclaimed the Chevalier, yawning with infinite content. Then he lay back in his bed, stared at the curious patterned canopy above him and nursed his waking thoughts.

He thought of the "Romaunt de la Rose", beautiful, but all too brief.

Of the Claude in Lady Delaware's collection.[1]

Of a wonderful pair of blonde trousers he would get Madame Belleville to make for him.

Of Saint Rose, the well known Peruvian virgin; how she vowed herself to perpetual virginity when she was four years old;[2] how she was beloved by Mary, who from the pale fresco in the Church of Saint Dominic, would stretch out her arms to embrace her; how she built a little oratory at the end of the garden and prayed and sang hymns in it till all the beetles, spiders, snails and creeping things came round to listen; how she promised to marry Ferdinand de Flores, and on the bridal morning perfumed herself and painted her lips, and put on her wedding frock, and decked her hair with roses, and went up to a little hill not far without the walls of Lima; how she knelt there some moments calling tenderly

---

[1] The *chef d'oeuvre*, it seems to me, of an adorable and impeccable master, who more than any other landscape-painter puts us out of conceit with our cities, and makes us forget the country can be graceless and dull and tiresome. That he should ever have been compared unfavourably with Turner — the Wiertz of landscape-painting — seems almost incredible. Corot is Claude's only worthy rival, but he does not eclipse or supplant the earlier master. A painting of Corot's is like an exquisite lyric poem, full of love and truth; whilst one of Claude's recalls some noble eclogue glowing with rich concentrated thought.

[2] "At an age," writes Dubonnet, "when girls are for the most part well confirmed in all the hateful practices of coquetry, and attend with gusto, rather than with distaste, the hideous desires and terrible satisfactions of men."
All who would respire the perfumes of Saint Rose's sanctity, and enjoy the story of the adorable intimacy that subsisted between her and Our Lady, should read Mother Ursula's "Ineffable And Miraculous Life Of The Flower Of Lima", published shortly after the canonisation of Rose by Pope Clement X in 1671.

"Truly," exclaims the famous nun, "to chronicle the girlhood of this holy virgin makes as delicate a task as to trace the forms of some slim, sensitive plant, whose lightness, sweetness, and simplicity defy and trouble the most cunning pencil." Mother Ursula certainly acquits herself of the task with wonderful delicacy and taste. A cheap reprint of the biography has lately been brought out by Chaillot and Son.

upon Our Lady's name, and how Saint Mary descended and kissed Rose upon the forehead and carried her swiftly into heaven.

He thought of the splendid opening of Racine's "Britannicus".

Of a strange pamphlet he had found in Venus' library, called "A Plea For The Domestication Of The Unicorn".

Of the "Bacchanals of Sporion".

Of love, and of a hundred other things.

Then his half-closed eyes wandered among the prints that hung upon the rose-striped walls. Within the delicate curved frames lived the corrupt and gracious creatures of Dorat and his school, slender children in masque and domino smiling horribly, exquisite lechers leaning over the shoulders of smooth doll-like girls and doing nothing in particular, terrible little Pierrots posing as lady lovers and pointing at something outside the picture, and unearthly fops and huge birdlike women mingling in some rococo room, lighted mysteriously by the flicker of a dying fire that throws great shadows upon wall and ceiling. One of the prints showing how an old Marquis practised the five-finger exercise, while in front of him his mistress offered her warm fesses to a panting poodle, made the Chevalier stroke himself a little.

Tannhäuser had taken some books to bed with him. One was the witty, extravagant "Tuesday And Josephine," another was the score of "Das Rheingold." Making a pulpit of his knees he propped up the opera before him and turned over the pages with a loving hand, and found it delicious to attack Wagner's brilliant comedy with the cool head of the morning. Once more he was ravished with the beauty and wit of the opening scene; the mystery of its prelude that seems to come up from the very mud of the Rhine, and to be as ancient, the abominable primitive wantonness of the music that follows the talk and movements of the Rhine-maidens, the black, hateful sounds in Alberich's love-making, and the flowing melody of the river of legends.[1]

But it was the third tableau that he applauded most that morning, the scene where Loge, like some flamboyant primeaval Scapin, practises his cunning upon Alberich. The feverish insistent ringing of the hammers at the forge, the dry staccato restlessness of Mime, the ceaseless coming and going of the troup of Nibelungs, drawn hither and thither like a flock of terror-stricken and infernal sheep, Alberich's savage activity and metamorphoses, and Loge's rapid, flaming, tonguelike movements, make the tableau the least reposeful, most troubled and confusing thing in the whole range of opera. How the Chevalier rejoiced in the extravagant monstrous poetry, the heated melodrama, and splendid agitation of it all!

At eleven o'clock Tannhäuser got up and slipped off his dainty night-dress, and postured elegantly before a long mirror, making much of himself. Now he would bend forward, now lie upon the floor, now stand upright, and now rest upon one leg and let the other hang loosely till he looked as if he might have been drawn by some early Italian master. Anon he would lie upon the floor with his back to the glass, and glance amorously over his shoulder. Then with a white silk sash he draped himself in a hundred charming ways. So engrossed was he with his mirrored shape that he had not noticed the entrance of a troop of serving boys, who stood admiringly but respectfully at a distance, ready to receive his waking orders. As soon as the Chevalier observed

---

[1] It is a thousand pities that concerts should only be given either in the afternoon, when you are torpid, or in the evening, when you are nervous. Surely you should assist at fine music as you assist at the Mass — before noon — when your brain and heart are not too troubled and tired with the secular influences of the growing day.

them he smiled sweetly, and bade them prepare his bath.

The bathroom was the largest and perhaps the most beautiful apartment in his splendid suite. The well-known engraving by Lorette that forms the frontispiece to Millevoye's "Architecture Du XVIIIᵉ Siècle" will give you a better idea than any words of mine of the construction and decoration of the room. Only in Lorette's engraving the bath sunk into the middle of the floor is a little too small.

Tannhäuser stood for a moment like Narcissus gazing at his reflection in the still scented water, and then just ruffling its smooth surface with one foot, stepped elegantly into the cool basin and swam round it twice very gracefully.

"Won't you join me?" he said, turning to those beautiful boys who stood ready with warm towels and perfume. In a moment they were free of their light morning dress, and jumped into the water and joined hands, and surrounded the Chevalier with a laughing chain.

"Splash me a little," he cried, and the boys teased him with water and quite excited him. He chased the prettiest of them and bit his fesses, and kissed him upon the perineum till the dear fellow banded like a carmelite, and its little bald top-knot looked like a great pink pearl under the water. As the boy seemed anxious to take up the active attitude, Tannhäuser graciously descended to the passive — a generous trait that won him the complete affections of his *valets de bain*, or pretty fish, as he liked to call them, because they loved to swim between his legs.

However, it is not so much at the very bath itself as in the drying and delicious frictions that a bather finds his chiefest joys, and Venus had appointed her most tried attendants to wait upon Tannhäuser. He was more than satisfied with their skill, and the delicate attention they paid his loving parts aroused feelings within him almost amounting to gratitude, and when the rites were ended any touch of homesickness he might have felt was utterly dispelled. After he had rested a little, and sipped his chocolate, he wandered into the dressing-room. Daucourt, his *valet de chambre*, Chenille, the perruquier and barber, and two charming young dressers, were awaiting him and ready with suggestions for the morning toilet. The shaving over, Daucourt commanded his underlings to step forward with the suite of suits from which he proposed Tannhäuser should make a choice. The final selection was a happy one. A dear little coat of pigeon rose silk that hung loosely about his hips, and showed off the jut of his behind to perfection; trousers of black lace in flounces, falling — almost like a petticoat — as far as the knee; and a delicate chemise of white muslin, spangled with gold and profusely pleated.

The two dressers, under Daucourt's direction, did their work superbly, beautifully, leisurely, with an exquisite deference for the nude, and a really sensitive appreciation of the Chevalier's scrumptious torso.

CHAPTER VIII

Of the ecstasy of Adolphe,
and the remarkable manifestation thereof

As pleased as Lord Foppington with his appearance, the
Chevalier tripped off to bid good-morning to Venus. He
found her in a sweet muslin frock, wandering upon the lawn,
and plucking flowers to deck her breakfast table. He kissed
her lightly upon the neck.

"I'm just going to feed Adolphe," she said, pointing to a
little reticule of buns that hung from her arm. Adolphe was
her pet unicorn. "He is such a dear," she continued; "milk
white all over excepting his nose, mouth, nostrils and John.
This way." The unicorn had a very pretty palace of its own,
made of green foliage and golden bars, a fitting home for
such a delicate and dainty beast. Ah, it was a splendid thing
to watch the white creature roaming in its artful cage, proud
and beautiful, knowing no mate, and coming to no hand
except the Queen's itself. As Tannhäuser and Venus
approached, Adolphe began prancing and curveting, pawing
the soft turf with his ivory hoofs and flaunting his tail like a
gonfalon. Venus raised the latch and entered.

"You mustn't come in with me, Adolphe is so jealous,"
she said, turning to the Chevalier, who was following her,

"but you can stand outside and look on, Adolphe likes an audience." Then in her delicious fingers she broke the spicy buns and with affectionate niceness breakfasted her snowy pet. When the last crumbs had been scattered, Venus brushed her hands together and pretended to leave the cage without taking any further notice of Adolphe. Every morning she went through this piece of play, and every morning the amorous unicorn was cheated into a distressing agony lest that day should have proved the last of Venus' love. Not for long, though, would she leave him in that doubtful, piteous state, but running back passionately to where he stood, made adorable amends for her unkindness.

Poor Adolphe! How happy he was, touching the Queen's breasts with his quick tongue-tip. I have no doubt that the keener scent of animals must make women much more attractive to them than to men; for the gorgeous odour that but faintly fills our nostrils must be revealed to the brute creation in divine fullness.

Anyhow, Adolphe sniffed as never a man did around the skirts of Venus. After the first charming interchange of affectionate delicacies was over, the unicorn lay down upon his side, and, closing his eyes, beat his stomach wildly with the mark of manhood.

Venus caught that stunning member in her hands and laid her cheek along it; but few touches were wanted to consummate the creature's pleasure. The Queen bared her left arm to the elbow, and with the soft underneath of it made amazing movements upon the tightly-strung instrument. When the melody began to flow, the unicorn offered up an astonishing vocal accompaniment. Tannhäuser was amused to learn that the etiquette of the Venusberg compelled everybody to await the outburst of these venereal sounds before they could sit down to *déjeuner*.

Adolphe had been quite profuse that morning.

Venus knelt where it had fallen, and lapped her little apéritif.

CHAPTER IX

*How Venus and Tannhäuser breakfasted
and then drove through the palace gardens*

The breakfasters were scattered over the gardens in *tête-à-têtes* and tiny parties. Venus and Tannhäuser sat together upon the lawn that lay in front of the Casino, and made havoc of a ravishing *déjeuner*. The Chevalier was feeling very happy. Everything around him seemed so white and light and matinal; the floating frocks of the ladies, the scarce-robed boys and satyrs stepping hither and thither elegantly, with meats and wines and fruits; the damask tablecloths, the delicate talk and laughter that rose everywhere; the flowers' colour and the flowers' scent; the shady trees, the wind's cool voice, and the sky above that was as fresh and pastoral as a perfect sixth. And Venus looked so beautiful.

"You're such a dear!" murmured Tannhäuser, holding her hand.

At the further end of the lawn, and a little hidden by a rose-tree, a young man was breakfasting alone. He toyed nervously with his food now and then, but for the most part leant back in his chair with unemployed hands, and gazed stupidly at Venus.

"That's Felix," said the Goddess, in answer to an enquiry

from the Chevalier;' and she went on to explain his attitude. Felix always attended Venus upon her little latrinal excursions, holding her, serving her, and making much of all she did. To undo her things, lift her skirts, to wait and watch the coming, to dip a lip or finger in the royal output, to stain himself deliciously with it, to lie beneath her as the favours fell, to carry off the crumpled, crotted paper — these were the pleasures of that young man's life.

Truly there never was a queen so beloved by her subjects as Venus. Everything she wore had its lover. Heavens! how her handkerchiefs were filched, her stockings stolen! Daily, what intrigues, what countless ruses to possess her merest frippery? Every scrap of her body was adored. Never, for Savaral, could her ear yield sufficient wax! Never, for Pradon, could she spit prodigally enough! And Saphius found a month an intolerable time.

After breakfast was over, and Felix's fears lest Tannhäuser should have robbed him of his capricious rights had been dispelled, Venus invited the Chevalier to take a more extensive view of the gardens, parks, pavilions, and ornamental waters. The carriage was ordered. It was a delicate, shell-like affair, with billowy cushions and a light canopy, and was drawn by ten satyrs, dressed as finely as the coachmen of the Empress Pauline the First.

The drive proved interesting and various, and Tannhäuser was quite delighted with almost everything he saw.

And who is not pleased when on either side of him rich lawns are spread with lovely frocks and white limbs — and upon flower-beds the dearest ladies are implicated in a glory of underclothing — when he can see in the deep cool shadow of the trees warm boys entwined, here at the base, there at the branch — when in the fountain's wave Love holds his court, and the insistent water burrows in every delicious crease and crevice?

A pretty sight, too, was little Rosalie, perched like a postilion upon the painted phallus god of all gardens. Her eyes were closed and she was smiling as the carriage passed. Round her neck and slender girlish shoulders there was a cloud of complex dress, over which bulged her wig-like flaxen tresses. Her legs and feet were bare, and the toes twisted in an amorous style. At the foot of the statue lay her shoes and stockings and a few other things.

Tannhäuser was singularly moved at this spectacle, and rose out of all proportion. Venus slipped the fingers of comfort under the lace flounces of his trousers, saying, "Is it all mine? Is it all mine?" and doing fascinating things. In the end, the carriage was only prevented from being overturned by the happy intervention of Mrs. Marsuple, who stepped out from somewhere or other just in time to preserve its balance.

How the old lady's eye glistened as Tannhäuser withdrew his panting blade! In her sincere admiration for fine things, she quite forgot and forgave the shock she had received from the falling of the gay equipage. Venus and Tannhäuser were profuse with apology and thanks, and quite a crowd of loving courtiers gathered round, consoling and congratulating in a breath.

The Chevalier vowed he would never go in the carriage again, and was really quite upset about it. However, after he had had a little support from the smelling-salts, he recovered his self-possession, and consented to drive on further.

The landscape grew rather mysterious. The park, no longer troubled and adorned with figures, was full of grey echoes and mysterious sounds; the leaves whispered a little sadly, and there was a grotto that murmured like a voice haunting the silence of a deserted oracle. Tannhäuser became a little triste. In the distance, through the trees, gleamed a still argent lake — a reticent, romantic water that must have held the subtlest fish that ever were. Around its marge the trees and flags and *fleurs de luce* were unbreakably asleep.

The Chevalier fell into a strange mood, as he looked at the lake. It seemed to him that the thing would speak, reveal some curious secret, say some beautiful word, if he should dare wrinkle its pale face with a pebble.

"I should be frightened to do that, though," he said to himself. Then he wondered what might be upon the other side; other gardens, other gods? A thousand drowsy fancies passed through his brain. Sometimes the lake took fantastic shapes, or grew to twenty times its size, or shrunk into a miniature of itself, without ever once losing its unruffled calm, its deathly reserve. When the water increased, the Chevalier was very frightened, for he thought how huge the frogs must have become. He thought of their big eyes and monstrous wet feet, but when the water lessened, he laughed to himself, whilst thinking how tiny the frogs must have grown. He thought of their legs that must look thinner than spiders', and of their dwindled croaking that never could be heard. Perhaps the lake was only painted, after all. He had seen things like it at the theatre. Anyway, it was a wonderful lake, a beautiful lake, and he would love to bathe in it, but he was sure he would be drowned if he did.

CHAPTER X

*Of the "Stabat Mater",
Spiridion and De La Pine*

When he woke up from his day-dreams, he noticed that the carriage was on its way back to the palace. They stopped at the Casino first, and stepped out to join the players at *petits chevaux*. Tannhäuser preferred to watch the game rather than play himself, and stood behind Venus, who slipped into a vacant chair and cast gold pieces upon lucky numbers. The first thing that Tannhäuser noticed was the grace and charm, the gaiety and beauty of the croupiers. They were quite adorable even when they raked in one's little losings. Dressed in black silk, and wearing white kid gloves, loose yellow wigs and feathered toques, with faces oval and young, bodies lithe and quick, voices silvery and affectionate, they made amends for all the hateful arrogance, disgusting aplomb, and shameful ugliness of the rest of their kind.

The dear fellow who proclaimed the winner was really quite delightful. He took a passionate interest in the horses, and had licked all the paint off their *petits couillons* !

You will ask me no doubt, "Is that all he did?" I will answer, "Not quite," as the merest glance at their *jolis derrières* would prove.

In the afternoon light that came through the great silken-blinded windows of the Casino, all the gilded decorations, all the chandeliers, the mirrors, the polished floor, the painted ceiling, the horses galloping round their green meadow, the fat rouleaux of gold and silver, the ivory rakes, the fanned and strange-frocked crowd of dandy gamesters looked magnificently rich and warm. Tea was being served. It was so pretty to see some plush little lady sipping nervously, and keeping her eyes over the cup's edge intently upon the slackening horses. The more indifferent left the tables and took their tea in parties here and there.

Tannhäuser found a great deal to amuse him at the Casino. Ponchon was the manager, and a person of extraordinary invention. Never a day but he was ready for a new show — a novel attraction. A glance through the old Casino programmes would give you a very considerable idea of his talent. What countless ballets, comedies, comedy-ballets, concerts, masques, charades, proverbs, pantomimes, *tableaux magiques*, and peep-shows *eccentriques*; what troupes of marionettes, what burlesques!

Ponchon had an astonishing flair for new talent, and many of the principal comedians and singers at the Queen's Theatre and Opera House had made their first appearance and reputation at the Casino.

This afternoon the *pièce de resistance* was a performance of Rossini's "Stabat Mater", an adorable masterpiece. It was given in the beautiful Salle des Printemps Parfumés. Ah! what a stunning rendering of the delicious *démodée pièce de décadence*. There is a subtle quality about the music, like the unhealthy bloom upon wax fruit, that both orchestra and singer contrived to emphasise with consummate delicacy.

The Virgin was sung by Spiridion, that soft, incomparable alto. A miraculous virgin, too, he made of her. To begin with, he dressed the role most effectively. His plump legs up to the feminine hips of him were in very white stockings clocked with a false pink. He wore brown kid boots, buttoned to mid-calf, and his whorish thighs had thin scarlet garters round them. His jacket was cut like a jockey's, only the sleeves ended in manifold frills, and round the neck, and just upon the shoulders there was a black cape. His hair, dyed green, was curled into ringlets, such as the smooth Madonnas of Morales are made lovely with, and fell over his high egg-shaped creamy forehead, and about his ears and cheeks and back.

The alto's face was fearful and wonderful — a dream face. The eyes were full and black, with puffy blue-rimmed hemispheres beneath them, the cheeks, inclining to fatness, were powdered and dimpled, the mouth was purple and curved painfully, the chin tiny, and exquisitely modelled, the expression cruel and womanish. Heavens! how splendid he looked and sounded.

An exquisite piece of phrasing was accompanied with some curly gesture of the hand, some delightful undulation of the stomach, some nervous movement of the thigh, or glorious rising of the bosom.

The performance provoked enthusiasm — thunders of applause. Claude and Clair pelted the thing with roses, and carried him off in triumph to the tables. His costume was declared ravishing. The men almost pulled him to bits, and mouthed at his great quivering bottom! The little horses were quite forgotten for the moment.

Sup, the penetrating, burst through his silk fleshings, and thrust in bravely up to the hilt, whilst the alto's legs were feasted upon by Pudex, Cyril, Anquetin, and some others. Ballice, Corvo, Quadra, Senillé, Mellefont, Théodore Le Vit, and Matta all of the egoistic cult, stood and crouched round, saturating the lovers with warm douches.

Later in the afternoon, Venus and Tannhäuser paid a little

visit to De La Pine's studio, as the Chevalier was very anxious to have his portrait painted. De La Pine's glory as a painter was hugely increased by his reputation as a *fouteur*, for ladies that had pleasant memories of him looked with a biased eye upon his *fêtes galantes merveilleuses*, portraits and *folies bergères*.

Yes, he was a bawdy creature, and his workshop a regular brothel. However, his great talent stood in no need of such meretricious and phallic support, and he was every whit as strong and facile with his brush as with his tool.

When Venus and the Chevalier entered his studio, he was standing amid a group of friends and connoisseurs who were liking his latest picture. It was a small canvas, one of his delightful morning pieces. Upon an Italian balcony stood a lady in a white frock, reading a letter. She wore brown stockings, straw-coloured petticoats, white shoes and a Leghorn hat. Her hair was red and in a chignon. At her feet lay a tiny Japanese dog, painted from the Queen's favourite "Fanny", and upon the balustrade stood an open empty bird cage. The background was a stretch of Gallic country, clusters of trees cresting the ridges of low hills, a bit of river, a château, and the morning sky.

De La Pine hastened to kiss the moist and scented hand of Venus. Tannhäuser bowed profoundly and begged to have some pictures shown him. The gracious painter took him round his studio.

Cosmé was one of the party, for De La Pine just then was painting his portrait, by the way, which promised to be a veritable *chef d'oeuvre*. Cosmé was loved and admired by everybody. To begin with, he was pastmaster in his art, that fine, relevant art of coiffing; then he was really modest and obliging, and was only seen and heard when he was wanted. He was useful; he was decorative in his white apron, black mask and silver suit; he was discreet.

The painter was giving Venus and Tannhäuser a little dinner that evening, and he insisted on Cosmé joining them. The barber vowed he would be *de trop*, and required a world of pressing before he would accept the invitation. Venus added her voice, and he consented.

Ah! what a delightful little *partie carrée* it turned out. The painter was in purple and full dress, all tassels and grand folds. His hair magnificently curled, his heavy eyelids painted, his gestures large and romantic, he reminded one a little of Maurel playing Wolfram in the second act of the Opera of Wagner.

Venus was in a ravishing toilet and confection of Camille's, and looked like K——. Tannhäuser was dressed as a woman and looked like a Goddess. Cosmé sparkled with gold, bristled with ruffs, glittered with bright buttons, was painted, powdered, gorgeously bewigged, and looked like a Marquis in a comic opera. The *salle à manger* at De La Pine's was quite the prettiest that ever was.

Also available:

BLOOD & ROSES

The Vampire in 19th Century Literature

Creation Classics

JOHN POLIDORI EDGAR ALLAN POE ARTHUR MACHEN
OSCAR WILDE SHERIDAN LE FANU LAUTRÉAMONT
BAUDELAIRE J. K. HUYSMANS BRAM STOKER
and many others

A definitive collection of 19th Century literature in which the
vampire, or vampirism, both embodied and atmospheric, appears.
Never before have these seminal texts, covering the whole range of
that period from Gothic and Romantic, through Symbolism and
proto-Surrealism to Decadence and beyond, appeared in one single,
comprehensive volume. The book is illustrated throughout with the
thanatopic/erotic works of Felicien Rops.

Large format, illustrated, £7.95 • $15.95

CRAWLING CHAOS
Selected Works 1920—1936
H P Lovecraft
Creation Classics

H P Lovecraft, one of the great obsessive writers of the 20th century, conjures a hideous universe lying just beyond our own; his relentless style and language forging a rich, convoluted literary form which ultimately achieves a veritable "pornography" of horror: the accumulation and repetition of his demonic visions climaxing in orgasms of cosmic revulsion.

Revolving around such mythical texts as *The Necronomicon*, the 23 stories in this volume comprise an essential, chronological collection of this unique writer's best work; from his early tales of the gruesome and bizarre, through his collaborative pieces and prose-poems, to the flowering of his personal cosmology, the *Cthulhu Mythos*.

With a brand new introduction by COLIN WILSON.
Large format, 368 pages, £9.95 • $19.95

THE GREAT GOD PAN
Arthur Machen
Creation Classics

First published in 1894, The Great God Pan is Arthur Machen's first, and greatest, opus of Decadence and Horror. With his singular eye for the bizarre and macabre, Machen unfurls this tale of a young girl cursed by her unnatural parentage.

This new, exclusive edition from Creation Books includes a set of complementary "automatic" drawings by Machen's contemporary and fellow mystic, **Austin Osman Spare**, as well as Machen's own illuminating introduction from the 1916 edition and a foreword by a leading member of the Arthur Machen Society with a comprehensive bibliography.

Large format, illustrated, £7.95 • $15.95

you have just read
salome & under the hill
a creation book
published by:
creation books
83, clerkenwell road, london ec1, uk
tel: 0171-430-9878 fax: 0171-242-5527
creation books is an independent publishing organisation producing
fiction and non-fiction genre books of interest to a young, literate
and informed readership.
*creation products should be available in all proper bookstores; please
ask your uk bookseller to order from:*
turnaround, 27 horsell road, london n5 1xl
tel: 0171-609-7836 fax: 0171-700-1205
non-book trade and mail order:
ak distribution, 22 lutton place, edinburgh eh8 9pe
tel: 0131-667-1507 fax: 0131-662-9594
readers in europe please order from:
turnaround distribution, 27 horsell road, london n5 1xl
tel: 0171-609-7836 fax: 0171-700-1205
readers in the usa please order from:
subterranean company, box 160, 265 south 5th street, monroe, or
97456
tel: 503 847-5274 fax: 503-847-6018
non-book trade and mail order:
ak press, po box 40682, san francisco, ca 94140-0682
tel: 415-923-1429 fax: 415-923-0607
readers in canada please order from:
marginal distribution, unit 102, 277 george street, n. peterborough,
ontario k9j 3g9
tel/fax: 705-745-2326
readers in australia and new zealand please order from:
peribo pty ltd, 58 beaumont road, mount kuring-gai, nsw 2080
tel: 02-457-0011 fax: 02-457-0022
readers in the rest of the world, or any readers having difficulty in
obtaining creation products, please order direct (+ 20% postage
outside uk) from our head office
our full mail order catalogue is available on request (please enclose
sae/2 ircs)
booksellers may order the full creation books trade catalogue free of
charge from any of the above addresses.